"*Resurrect* is high adventu.......g......... tradition, with a brash hero, relentless villains, beautiful women, and breathtaking locales from the Himalaya to Hong Kong. It is as addictive as hot buttered popcorn—you'll keep coming back for more."
—Stephen M. Irwin, award-winning author of *The Dead Path* and *The Broken Ones*

"Resurrect by Kane Gilmour is a smart, taut thriller that takes the genre forged by Clive Cussler and makes it fresh again. The combination of history, conspiracy and explosive action makes the book impossible to put down. Highly recommended!"
—Jeremy Robinson, bestselling author of *Secondworld* and *Island 731*

"If you're a fan of thrillers, and you haven't read Kane Gilmour's *Resurrect*, you need your head examined. Quickly. Gilmour mixes Clive Cussler with Matthew Reilly, then adds a healthy dose of his own style. The result is a debut novel that stands with the best in the genre and leaves you ready to pound on Gilmour's door demanding the sequel."
—Edward G. Talbot, author of *2012: The Fifth World* and *New World Orders*

"I know I'm not the first to say it, but it bears repeating. Kane Gilmour has tapped into the same creative vein that energized Clive Cussler's earlier Dirk Pitt novels. It's all there, from the pitch-perfect character chemistry to over-the-top action. If you've been craving some old school Cussler, you really need to read *Resurrect*."
—Sean Ellis, author of *Dark Trinity: Ascendent* and *Wargod*

"*Resurrect* is a thriller teeming with action-adventure goodness: an intriguing historical mystery, a tough and resourceful hero, a dangerous villain, and a globe-hopping adventure filled with chases, escapes, and action to spare."
—David Wood, author of *Dark Rite* and *Buccaneer*

Praise for *The Crypt of Dracula*

"All the hallmarks of a great, 1970s classic creature flick are here: spooky castle, the gentleman creature of the night, and harried villagers poised to grab pitchforks and torches. Gilmour brings Dracula back, with a dash of 21st century adventure and a twist you won't see coming."

—Jeremy Bishop, #1 bestselling horror author of *Torment* and *The Sentinel*

"*The Crypt of Dracula* is how a vampire novel should be written. It's suspenseful, frightening, dark, and realistic. It harkens back to the day when 'monster' movies played at Saturday matinees and at midnight showings. Somewhere, Bram Stoker is smiling. He's beaming from ear to ear because someone finally got it right, and that someone is Kane Gilmour."

—Suspense Magazine

"If you are a fan of the old-style Dracula stories, you will definitely enjoy reading *The Crypt of Dracula*. Kane did an amazing job recreating the feel of Stoker while adding his own style. Travel to a magnificent castle perched dangerously on a cliff in Romania, with a very dark and dangerous secret. Within the walls hide your worst nightmares, blood-thirsty and evil. Finally, a vampire that makes you weak in the knees and afraid of the dark. There are definitely no *emo*, glittering vampires in this book! Be prepared to sleep with the lights on."

—Carol 'Pixie' Brearley, author of *Rise of the Dark Angel* and *Dark Wings Spread*

"Experience the Count again...for the first time! Gilmour's version of Dracula is both homage to the classic Hammer films and a re-imagining that will have you peeking out your covers at night, while at the same time giggling like Renfield with each turn of the page. Don't let the sun go down before getting this awesome book!"

—J. Kent Holloway, author of *Devil's Child* and *The Curse of One-Eyed Jack*

THE CRYPT OF
DRACULA

Also By Kane Gilmour

The Jason Quinn Series
Resurrect
Frozen (coming in 2013)

The Monster Kingdom Series
Monster Kingdom (coming in 2013)

Horror & Fantasy
The Crypt of Dracula
Interstate 0 (with J. Kent Holloway) (coming in 2013)

Jeremy Robinson's Jack Sigler / Chess Team Series
Callsign: Deep Blue (with Jeremy Robinson)
Ragnarok (with Jeremy Robinson)
Omega (with Jeremy Robinson) (coming in 2013)

Edited Anthology
Warbirds of Mars: Stories of the Fight!
(Edited by Scott P. Vaughn & Kane Gilmour)

THE CRYPT OF DRACULA

KANE GILMOUR

Illustrations by Scott P. Vaughn

Quickdraw Books

Visit Kane Gilmour on the World Wide Web at:
www.kanegilmour.com

Visit Christian Troels Tromsø Guldager on the World Wide Web at:
www.chrisguldager.com

Visit Scott P. Vaughn on the World Wide Web at:
www.vaughn-media.com

For Timothy Louis Conley,
and his love of vampire movies—
good, bad, and absurdly terrible.

FOREWORD

Why Dracula? Isn't he a little passé in 2013? Isn't this Gilmour guy supposed to be a thriller author? What's he doing writing horror?

Well, yes, okay. Fair enough. But even thriller authors have other interests, and who doesn't find a really good, old-fashioned spookfest like Dracula thrilling? This novella happened because of my love for all things old and spooky. As a child of the 1970s, I grew up watching the old Universal monster pictures on TV, late Saturday mornings and Sunday afternoons, after the cartoons were over. When I could, I also watched the Hammer horror flicks that came on late at night. In fact, my first memory of ever seeing a horror film was Hammer's *Scars of Dracula* with Christopher Lee as the Count, seen through mostly closed eyelids, as I pretended to be asleep for the babysitter. I think I was four. Yes, you read that right. At age four, I was watching an obviously rubber bat vomit neon-red blood onto a desiccated corpse in a coffin, and loving every bloody minute of it. I was instantly hooked on the Count and all things spooky.

The 1970s were a great time for it, too—you could get your spookables in toys, comics, books, on the radio, on television (live action and animated), in films, on records, and even in breakfast cereals. I suppose around the age of thirteen, I must have actually read the original Bram Stoker story, but I confess to not remembering much of it (until I read it again, years later). Although the tale holds up well, it isn't quite so accessible to a thirteen-year-old boy—even one who loves Dracula from other mediums—as English teachers always like to think. Instead, my vision of the Count is, and has always been, an absolute mish-mash of hundreds of films (most bad), and countless televisions shows. (Although I'm rediscovering Stoker again now, and find I'm enjoying the story far more than I ever could have as a pre-teen.)

So why this story, and why as a novella? Well, it's all the fault of two of my very talented friends. Scott 'Doc' Vaughn has been a friend since the mid 1990s, and he's also the artist that did the lush interior illustrations for this little tale. He's also one of the biggest film buffs I've ever known, and he has an extensive collection of older films. He and I got talking in 2011 about horror films, because I had been reading some really great supernatural horror novels by names like Joe Hill and Michael Koryta. Their stories whetted my appetite for more, and I turned to Doc for advice on some old films to check out. I wanted some oldies but goodies that I might never have seen. Doc's gonna come back into this story in a bit, but for now, just know that he pointed me at some great films, and I started watching and re-watching a lot of the classics.

I had another great supernatural horror book, too. I had picked up a book by an Australian writer named Stephen M. Irwin. Within a few chapters, I was ready to put him in the category of literary heir to Stephen King, right next to Koryta and King's actual heir, Joe Hill. Irwin can construct a devastatingly lovely sentence, and he can invoke your gleefully misspent youth one minute and the next he pulls your darkest terror from your soul, the way some clawed beast might tear your heart from your chest. I started talking about Irwin to my friends, and in a short time, through the wonders of the Internet, Steve and I became online friends. We share a love of short stories, the supernatural, and as we came to discover, of film. Steve was doing a series of posts on his Facebook page about the top films of each decade (of his life) that influenced him personally and creatively, and I responded with my own lists. *Scars of Dracula*, it should come as no surprise, was on my list for the 1970s. The lists made me really think about the films, and why and how they had influenced me. Thinking about all the early horror films I had watched and loved, and distilling them down to their essence (and choosing so few, so there would be room for other genres in my lists) was challenging, but it woke something in me. My love of that era of creature stories came rushing back to the surface.

So I'm blaming Doc and Steve. They encouraged me and got my head spinning around my nostalgic love for the classic monster genre of horror, and the more I thought about it, the more I fondly remembered those older tales. The more the era flitted through my head, the more I began to contrast those stories with the modern attempts to re-create the vampire, and often to make vampires the object of teen and pre-teen girl fantasy. I realized that many of my old favorites were in the public domain, and available for reinterpretation—or for a nostalgic re-creation. A few short novellas featuring Dracula and a few featuring Frankenstein's creature might be just the thing to work it out of my system, but they would need to be faithful to my mish-mashed recollections, informed by decades of film, comics, books, and TV shows.

I started talking with Doc about it, and he thought it would be a good idea. He thought the stories would work pretty well as a series of novellas—he even signed on for interior illustrations on this one. I talked with the immensely creative Christian Guldager, who, from his secret base under a volcano in Denmark, geeked over the idea and came up with more sketches for the cover than he could actually paint. I think you'll agree that his cover evokes the smoldering stare of the Count quite nicely.

So I had cool art; I had a killer cover. I had a purpose and a direction. I just needed one last thing, and Doc provided it. He observed, quite succinctly summing up what I was having difficulty putting into words, that what was missing from the vampire stories of today were *the rules*. The rules governing what a vampire could and couldn't do, and also those prescribing how to kill one. As soon as Doc said it, I recognized how right he was. What was missing from stories about sparkly teenagers with moody pouts was the implacable will of instinct. It was the sheer menace of a man who attempted to maintain a fine veneer of civility and charm, but who was, in secret and just barely under the surface, a true creature governed by his instincts. He was absolutely a victim to them, just as those he preyed upon were victims of his hunger.

Dracula, the real Count Dracula, was not just a man or a vampire. He wasn't a sexy plaything for lusty women. He was an animal, shaped like a man. A beast, completely unable to control himself at the sight of a slit wrist. He had to *feed*, man.

So that was my mandate, to my friends and to myself: to present a simple, nostalgic tale of Dracula, following some rules, and staying true to what made him great. Is this story a direct sequel to Stoker's tale? No. Does it follow every aspect of Stoker's creation exactly? Again, no. Is it the vampire tale to reinvent vampires for the 21st century? Nope. Am I trying to set the world on fire here? No. The Dracula in this story is the same Count as in every other tale. You *know* him. He might look a little different here. He's younger than the old Romanian rattling around his empty castle in Stoker's tale, pretending he was every one of his nonexistent staff. He's more verbose than Christopher Lee ever was, but he certainly doesn't prattle like that old man in Stoker's novel, either. He has the smolder in his eyes, but he doesn't ever give us the exaggerated linguistic struggle and melodramatic movements of my beloved Béla Lugosi.

The Crypt of Dracula takes liberties with the geography of Romania (Transylvania was technically a part of Hungary at the time) and with that of Stoker's novel, which are not always one and the same. I make the characters follow some rules, but I also do not. You'll recognize the setting—a crumbling old castle on a cliffside. You'll know the nearby village, and you'll see the reluctance of the villagers to get involved. Because they *know*. You won't know the names of the hero or the supporting cast. They're new. But you know their roles. Some will live and some will die. And you know, you just *know*, that someone is going to stake that crazy bloodsucking bastard through the heart by the end. The fun will be seeing how it all plays out.

Kane Gilmour
Montpelier, April 2013

PROLOGUE

Southeast of the Borgo Pass, Hungary, 1897

Lightning crackled horizontally across the sky, throwing the ruined castle into a stark contrast with the suddenly illuminated heavens.

"Storms come on very suddenly in the mountains, I'm afraid," the solicitor said, while struggling with the lock on the banded wooden door. The roar of the thunder, following the flash, drowned out the latter part of his apology.

"No need to trouble yourself, setting our minds at rest, sir. We are familiar with the weather, and I can assure you, the climate will hold little sway over my decision whether to purchase the property. We are simply grateful you could take the time to show it to us." Thin, and over six and a half feet tall, Dragos Petran exuded all the Oxford charm he could toward the reluctant solicitor. His lovely wife, Alina, stood beside him and smiled widely, although she had privately expressed her reservations about Petran's plans for the property. The crumbling castle on a crag some seven thousand feet above sea level was an unusual spot, and the nearest village was a few miles away by coach. Still, she had agreed to come and inspect the site with him, and Petran was pleased at her willingness.

"Ah, here we are." The solicitor shoved the wooden door with his shoulder. It creaked inward. His grin looked sheepish at the sad state of the ruined grounds and the groaning door, but Petran was unperturbed. The solicitor slipped inside and before Petran and his wife were fully in the doorway, the portly man was returning from the interior gloom with a lighted candlestick. "Although the exterior needs some work, you'll find the design work inside is top-notch, and the furniture and fittings are all well appointed."

Petran helped the slender Alina to shed her overcoat, and he hung it on a dark wooden coat rack just inside the heavy door. The solicitor moved around the room and lit additional candles. Soon the room was filled with a warm yellow glow, and Petran could see the fine woodwork in the large hall, and the long-since-faded tapestries. An enormous curved marble staircase swept up to a darkened second story. Short hallways led off in every direction on the ground floor. A thick Persian rug covered most of the floor, but Petran could see the black and white checked marble at the edges of the vast foyer.

"It's lovely," Alina said, and Petran could tell she was sincere, as he had instructed her to be.

"The castle was owned by a local Count for many years, and I believe it was in his family for a few hundred years. He was a businessman who traveled abroad widely, but he mysteriously disappeared on one such trip. As you can see, the grounds have fallen into disrepair."

"How long has the property been vacant?" Petran asked.

"Well, we've had a caretaker on the grounds a few times in the last years, of course, but the Count went missing over seven years ago now." The man spoke calmly, as he led them through the ground floor rooms, lighting candles as he went, to dispel the dense shadows. Petran noticed that the older man showed no more hesitation or awkwardness. Now inside the building, the man had slipped into a routine he had no doubt undergone countless times. Petran knew the castle had been on the Agency's listings of available properties for the last four years, and that this solicitor had shown the crumbling estate to several prospective buyers who had passed on the opportunity. Soon there would be no more prospective buyers—but not because Petran planned to buy the castle. He had other plans.

The man led them through the huge kitchen, one hand clutching the candlestick and the other mopping sweat off his brow with a fine linen handkerchief. Petran wondered if the solicitor could somehow sense that something was wrong with the castle, every time the man led his clients here. On the surface, the man seemed fine, but Petran suspected that deep inside the solicitor's brain, some instinctual lobe that governed self-preservation was bursting with energy, trying to warn the sweaty little man. But after several visits to the secluded castle, he must have learned to ignore that feeling.

"Shall we move upstairs next?" The man spoke to Alina, who had showed the most interest in the immense kitchen.

Petran stepped forward. "Is there a wine cellar? I would like to see that first, I should think. Also to inspect the foundations of the structure." Petran looked around himself as he spoke, acting disinterested. He was making the chubby man work hard for a sale that would never happen.

"Certainly, sir." The man led them to a painted white, wooden door on the edge of the kitchen that revealed a wide stone stairwell, which curved gently downward into a broad spiral. Each step was cut from a massive slab of smooth stone, and Petran wondered whether the rock had been hewn directly from the mountain. The solicitor led the way, lighting sconces as he descended the broad steps. Alina followed him, daintily crossing each step with three strides for every one Petran needed to cross the slabs, as he followed her.

The rooms in the lower section of the castle were endless, but most were empty, standing solitary along the curving stairwell wall like dark prison cells. Petran simply popped his head in each as the rotund solicitor swept past them to the lower reaches, buried deep inside the mountain. At the bottom, the man moved into the wide room with a flourish. His candlelight jumped and leapt to the high stone arches of the chamber.

"Oh my," Alina breathed.

Petran scanned the darker recesses of nooks and indents in the walls. Each was filled with rack after rack of dusty wine bottles. They looked French, but Petran was suspicious of the contents. Still, he would make no comment.

"The wine cellar is fully stocked, as you can see, and would, of course, be included in the price, sir." The solicitor looked pleased with himself. The arrangement of the multitude of wine racks formed a kind of labyrinth, with twisting alleys between the rows and rows of bottles.

Petran strode past the man winding his way through the racks of bottles, acting as if he were appraising them and their potential value. He made his way toward the distant back of the chamber and muttered under his breath. "For so many Swiss Francs, I should hope so." He was loud enough that the other man could hear him, but just barely. "And what is back here?"

Petran stopped at a locked door at the back of the cellar.

"I believe it is only a root cellar." The solicitor was on his way back to the stairs to the kitchen. "Shall we move up?"

"We've come all this way, sir. I feel I would be remiss if I did not inspect every room, else I would have wasted your time." Petran smiled in the shadows as the solicitor reluctantly returned through the arches. By the time the man's candlelight reached him through the maze of dusty wooden racks, Petran's face had returned to a neutral and somewhat disinterested visage. Alina joined them, but she looked disappointed. Petran could see she had no interest in a potential root cellar, and she had been eager to follow the solicitor up the spiral stairs. Petran wondered if she could feel it, too. The raw menace of the place.

He stepped aside to allow the sweaty man to unlock the wide door, with a key from his ring of metal keys. The jingling filled the dimly lit space with an outlandish and unwelcome cheerfulness. Petran gave Alina a reassuring smile.

They stepped inside the chamber, Petran ducking his head slightly under the doorframe, and the solicitor drew a sharp breath. The yellow light illuminated a small space with a stone coffin on a raised platform in its exact center, its head toward the door. The room was otherwise empty.

"It's a tomb!" The man was clearly befuddled. Petran had suspected that the man would never have been in the room, but now he was certain.

"A crypt, sir. Let us see who is buried here." Petran stepped forward toward the coffin.

"I don't think we should—"

Petran drowned out his wife's tiny voice by demanding the solicitor help him with the stone lid. The small man harrumphed, but moved forward and did as he was told. The lid was heavy, but the two men were easily able to slide it aside, and then lift it and gently place it on the floor. Alina moved up with the two men as all three peered into the depths of the coffin. The flickering light made the small pile of ashes look golden, but Petran knew they would be gray in daylight. The thought was moot. They were about to become a different color.

Petran stepped back slightly, and in one fluid movement, removed the large carving knife from his jacket. He had picked it up in the kitchen before they descended the spiral stair. One hand reached around the portly solicitor's face from behind, and the other brought the silver blade sweeping across the man's throat.

Blood erupted from the man's neck, spraying the ashen contents of the coffin as his body went limp.

Alina screamed when she saw the solicitor's life pool into the stone sarcophagus. She stumbled back, away from the blood and the coffin. Petran looked at her and saw in her eyes that she understood she would be next. He dropped the corpse on the coffin and stepped toward his young bride. Her eyes widened at his approach, but then they darted quickly back to the coffin, and the horror that waited there.

When her eyes widened further still, Petran knew what was happening behind him. He lunged forward as Alina turned and ran, his long legs easily closing the distance between them as she darted left and right through the twisting maze of wine racks, until he cornered her at a dead end, against a stone wall.

"You should be *honored*," he whispered in her ear, as he dragged her thrashing form back to the waiting coffin.

He didn't want to miss the sight, and he had already missed much of it. Under the solicitor's flaccid form, a body now filled the coffin, where before there had been only ash. Although 'body' was a bit optimistic. Petran could see bone in places, and veins and arteries networking the form. Muscle was growing. Skin, however, was still entirely missing. Alina fainted in his clutches.

Petran wasted no time. He grabbed her by her long hair before her body reached the floor. He yanked her skull up and over the lip of the coffin's sidewall and then brought the blade smoothly across her neck, exactly as he had done with the fat man. More blood sprayed into the container, and skin began to grow over the skeleton's muscles before Petran's eyes.

The process took less than half an hour.

When the man sat up and climbed out of the coffin, Petran dropped to his knees.

"Welcome back, my Lord." Petran spoke now in Hungarian, instead of in English.

The man in front of the sarcophagus stood slightly taller than six feet, with long, shoulder-length black hair on his head, but none anywhere else on his nude form. His skin was a pasty white, and Petran could see bluish veins through the transparent flesh. He was surprised how young the man looked. No more than thirty years, if a day. The man's eyes smoldered with a fire that spoke of years of anguish and a dire need for revenge.

Petran thought of the being before him as a man, but he soon learned his mistake.

The creature hissed at him and bared its teeth.

"I still thirst," it said, with a throaty croak.

Petran hung his head in stark disappointment.

"I understand."

Petran, still on his knees on the hard stone floor, closed his eyes as the creature descended on him. It sank its teeth into his neck, long fangs puncturing the skin. As Petran's blood began to flow, the creature sank its teeth deeper.

And drank.

CHAPTER ONE

Dorna-Velta, Hungary, 1899

Andreas Wagner stepped down from the coach and took in the bleak little village around him. The buildings were all white-washed structures, tightly grouped together around the central road that ran through the village, with narrow winding alleys off to the sides. Some of the buildings had thatched roofs and some had farm equipment parked or abandoned in front of them, rusting in the elements. The buildings all appeared to lean into toward each other, as if shivering from too many brutal Carpathian winters.

The sky was a billowing explosion of dark autumn clouds threatening to dump torrents on him at any second. The few trees around the village were tangled and dark, and the hills were so thick that he could see little past the first range of them. Small farm fields with distinctive pear-shaped haystacks on poles circled the tiny hovels and the single crumpled church in the town. But he had noticed larger untilled fields that ringed the smaller active ones, on his journey in. The dead fields looked like a barrier, announcing his crossing into civilization, after long hours in the coach.

Wagner could see no villagers anywhere on the fields or amongst the tightly grouped buildings. The growing wind banged a loose shutter on the window of one of the tiny houses, the sound a steady *clack* on the wind.

Last stop before the castle, Wagner thought. *A pitiful place.*

The wind blew hard, making his long, thick blonde hair dance on the currents. He ran a hand through his mane, attempting to keep bits of it from whipping him in the eyes. He stretched his lower back, twisting and turning the kinks out after the long ride from the spa town of Dorna-Watra. He reached down to touch his toes, then stood and turned to face the driver up on the coach. The man was reclined on the driver's seat, a small flask clutched in his hand. He was already sound asleep, even though the coach had stopped only a moment before. *It's a wonder we made it here at all.*

Deciding to let the old man sleep it off, Wagner stepped toward the town's only inn, hoping the place would have a beer and a warm meal. Then he would decide whether to press on to the castle as night fell or wait until the following morning.

He had no reservations about having taken the job. He needed the money, and this job promised plenty. More, though, he needed a new start. Everyone and everything in Munich had been getting on his nerves. He understood why, but in the moment, he could blame it all on Munich and Germany in general. In his soul, and in his quieter moments of reflection, he knew that the death of his infant child the previous year was the cause of all of his mood swings. *Britta. My little Britta.*

She had died of some inexplicable wasting disease. None of the doctors could even pose any theories on what had taken his precious little six-month-old darling from him. *They were useless.* His wife, Anneli, was unable to even speak afterwards. It had been a year and both of them had grieved enough. Her moods were generally improving and far cheerier than he had seen from her in a long time. She was taking her pleasures in small things like planting flowers in the small garden of their place in Munich. Her voice had not returned yet, but her disposition had.

Wagner was the opposite. At first he raged and raged until his voice was hoarse. Now his voice had grown silent, as he brewed internally, wanting change but not knowing how to accomplish it.

He talked only when he needed to, and his disposition leaned more toward long silences and lack of emotion now, than toward anger.

Still, things had been improving with the two of them, and they had even begun lovemaking again. He supposed that their relationship would have eventually been restored with time, and maybe her voice would return as well. The doctors all told him that the loss of her vocal abilities was strictly psychological. A specialist had traveled from Vienna to examine her, and the man had given Wagner much the same impression. His wife would speak again, but not until she was ready.

Then Wagner had received the letter.

A new chance for a start, in a distant land, working for an eccentric noble. It sounded too good to be true. But Wagner had begun shutting down his life and work as a well-respected stonemason and craftsman in Munich. He would come here to the distant reaches of the Carpathian Mountains, meet the noble, and begin work on the restoration of the man's gigantic home. In a few weeks, once things were settled and Wagner had had time to prepare their quarters, his wife would make the long journey from Munich to Vienna, then on to Budapest and Klausenburg, and finally through Bistritz and into the mountains past the Borgo Pass and the tiny vacation town with the ski resorts north of him. She would come here—Wagner looked around—to this desolate forgotten village, and join him at last.

Wagner looked again to the door of the inn, its bright green paint fading and peeling.

Let's hope the people are warmer than the landscape.

As he stepped up to the door, he failed to notice the large silver cross, nailed above the doorframe.

CHAPTER TWO

Silence fell as the door to the tavern opened.

Wagner had heard talking and merriment through the heavy wooden door before he had opened it, but now the room had fallen quiet. He had been in plenty of drinking establishments in Germany, and many of them in small insular villages fell silent when newcomers stepped inside. But in those cases, the silence was from curiosity as the locals looked over newcomers. As Wagner moved into the room, he looked around and saw most people not meeting his eye, or even looking in his direction. They weren't curious, or even angry. They looked like they were hoping he wouldn't notice they were there.

The room had a low ceiling with dark exposed beams. A few local crafts were colorfully decorating the walls along with a very large crucifix, which Wagner thought odd for a tavern. Was the place used for worship on Sundays, because of the disheveled state of the village's church? There were small tables and chairs around the room, and many men crowded throughout it. They all looked to be locals, wearing the customary shirts and woolen sweaters he had seen in countless villages on his travel through the region. Hard-working farm folk. Normally, the kind of people Wagner thought of as *his kind of folk*. But not these people. They all seemed shriveled and shrunken. Hoping not to be noticed. Hiding their faces in the tops of their beer steins. Looking away as he walked in the room.

As if they were all frightened of something.

A pretty waitress in a dress bustled out of the room with her tray, into what Wagner supposed would be the kitchen. At a counter that served as both reception and a bar, a middle-aged man with hair plastered down on his head in a greasy smear stood drying a glass with a white rag. His gray eyes avoided Wagner's, as if he, too, were hoping the stranger would just find the room too inhospitable and just leave. At least the fireplace emitted some warmth, even if the people did not. Wagner wouldn't be going anywhere until his fingers were warmer and his back was unkinked.

"Do you have a room?" Wagner asked the innkeeper.

The man finally looked up at him, wariness in his glare. "Where are you heading, sir?"

"The castle. I was thinking of spending the night here, though, and pressing on in the morning."

"There's no castle near here," the man said, and began wiping the glass again, as if the conversation was over.

"I'm told it's just a few miles south and east of here. You must know it." Wagner was surprised the man wouldn't know about the place. He suspected the man was lying. It was there in his demeanor and his pinched face.

Upon hearing the directions, though, the man stopped his polishing and looked up. Color, what little there was, had drained from the man's face. "Why would you want to go there? That place is abandoned."

"Oh, but it isn't. I've been hired to make repairs to the structure. I'm a stone mason, you see."

"Hired?" The innkeeper raised one bushy eyebrow. "By whom?"

Andreas looked stunned. Surely these people must know his employer. "By Count Dracula."

CHAPTER THREE

The greasy innkeeper swallowed hard, an audible click in his throat. Someone else in the packed room had gasped in a breath at the mention of the name. Wagner turned his head and took in the smoky room again. All eyes were facing his way now, and they all showed fear.

"We haven't heard that name in some time, sir. We had heard that the Count was dead." Wagner turned back to see the innkeeper had begun to sweat at the top of his slick forehead.

"Well, I received a letter from the Count, asking if I would come work for him to restore his castle. He did mention that he had been away for several years, and that the place had fallen into some disrepair. He said he is a businessman. Do you know what sort of work he does?"

"As long as he does his business abroad, we don't really care." The innkeeper said, and turned to a wooden board behind him, pulling down a large brass key. "Room 3 is available. You should definitely stay the night. The road to the castle is…treacherous at night. Much safer in the daylight."

The man sounded angry now, and Wagner wondered if he had perhaps lost loved ones on the road to the castle. He would have to speak to the Count about it, and if need be, maybe he could be further employed to shore up the dangerous road. It would be a lengthy job and would keep him paid for a long while, well after the castle restoration project was done. Wagner had worked some simple road jobs in Bavaria, and he was familiar with the twisting, crumbling roads in the mountain passes.

"Andreas Wagner," he said, taking the key from the man.

"I am Martin Miklos. This inn is my home." The man shook Wagner's hand, and then went back to polishing his glass, this time with a defeated resignation about him.

"A pleasure," Wagner told him. "Would I be able to get a warm meal as well?"

"The girl will bring you some food," Miklos said, then he set the glass down and clapped his hands loudly.

The brunette waitress with long curling hair and a large bosom squeezed into a tight fitting dress, reappeared from the kitchen, and Miklos pointedly nodded his head at Wagner. She slipped back into the kitchen, her long curls bouncing. Miklos turned back to Wagner. "Take a seat, sir."

Wagner turned to walk to the only available seat, at a table with three other men, one drinking his beer quickly, and a younger man just staring down at the table. The third was an older man. He was smoking a Bavarian pipe that filled the corner of the room with a deep fragrance. Then Wagner remembered the coach driver and turned back to Miklos.

"Oh. The coach man is passed out on his seat—he'll likely need a bed for the night as well."

A tall man leaning by the door, holding a stein filled to the brim with beer and squinting out the sole window in the room, turned to Wagner. "No. He's already left."

"What?" Wagner raced over to the window. "He was supposed to take me on to the castle!" He moved to the door and opened it, only to find his luggage deposited on the hard ground outside. He stepped over the bags and out into the dark dirt road. He peered into the distance and could just make out the coach moving around a curve in the road, deeper into the forest, back toward the north.

"Blast! What will I do?" Wagner reached down and picked up his bags, bringing them back into the tavern.

Miklos had stepped away from the bar and came now to close the door firmly, once Wagner was in, locking it with three locks from the inside. He reached out to take Wagner's bags and said, "I imagine the Count will send his own coach for you, if he is really back, as you say."

The man moved with the bags toward the stairs, and Wagner slipped into his seat at the table. The others had not moved from their places. The man with the pipe slid a stein of beer toward Wagner, then nodded to him. "You sound like you are from Bavaria, Herr Wagner."

"Yes." Wagner took a deep pull from his stein.

"I came from there many years ago," said the man. "You'll find that most of the people in Transylvania are deeply superstitious, and that coach drivers are not to be relied upon, as they are in other parts of the world."

"So I see."

The conversation was minimal, and eventually the food came, the waitress weaving through the tightly spaced tables with her tray, while fending off leers. The meal was a thick stew with cabbage, potatoes, and meat. A huge loaf of bread was provided, as well as succulent cheese and grapes bursting with flavor. Wagner thought he might not have eaten so well in many years. The people were strange in this village, and the landscape was bleak and foreboding, but he had never had food so good.

At one point, Wagner asked the Bavarian man whether the tavern was full every night.

"Yes. This is the entire village," the man told him, between puffs on his pipe.

"Where are all the women and children?"

Miklos, who had overheard the conversation while walking by, answered loudly. "They are safe."

The conversation died down after that, and most of the men resumed their gloomy stares into the depths of their steins or their own bowls of steaming stew. An older man in the corner with a long, flowing white beard had his head bowed down, as if asleep. Others were drinking with stern faces, lost in their individual thoughts. Wagner wanted to inquire about what kind of construction supplies he might find in the village, because he knew he would likely need to make many trips down from the castle, but with the mood as grim as it was, he figured he had best wait until morning. When he was done with his beer and stew, he made his polite excuses and retired to his tiny room at the top of the stairs. After laying down on the soft mattress, he was asleep in moments.

As Wagner left the room, all eyes in the tavern followed him.

Miklos watched him trudge up the stairs and waited for the sound of the guest room door shutting. After a few moments, Miklos turned back to his fellow villagers. He dismissed the waitress for the night, and after she had left the room, he spoke to the others.

"Unbelievable. He's back."

Henning Brandt, the German who had spoken with Wagner, took a large puff on his pipe and spoke loudly so the others would hear—but not so loudly that the blonde stranger might hear from upstairs. "We knew there was a possibility."

Nicolai Razvan, a hefty and morose farmer in the corner, spoke next. "What should we do? Few of us have remained these long years. I cannot part with my family land. If…he's really back?"

Miklos frowned at Razvan's refusal to speak the Count's name. Most of the villagers refused to utter it, out of some irrational fear that it would summon him from his castle to their doorstep. "I will tell you what we'll do—"

"You will do nothing." The old man spoke sharply from the corner of the room. His head had been bowed for most of the evening, as if he were asleep, or at least in deep concentration. His long, flowing white hair and beard obscured the thick starched collar hidden under it. The priest with the thick German accent had always commanded respect, even before he was a man of the cloth. Now he raised his head and looked into the room at each man, pointedly, until no one could hold his gaze. His pale blue eyes—almost white, Miklos thought—burned with a strange, fiery hatred that Miklos had not seen in the old man for a long time.

Not since the last time.

"You will all do nothing," the priest said again, struggling to stand before limping around the room. "We will let Herr Wagner make his way to the castle, and we will gather information. We will determine whether the Count is truly returned, or if Herr Wagner's new employer is some pretender to the throne of evil. Once we have sufficient information...*I* will act." The priest stalked around the small space, weaving between the tables as he spoke, and every man present, whether devout or not, deferred to the raging fires in the normally contemplative pastor.

The stress and authority in the man's voice clearly conveyed that *he* would be in charge of any organized reaction to the Count's return.

"And if the killings begin again?" Miklos asked.

A gleam of danger brewed in the ancient priest's eyes as he turned his gaze on Miklos. "Well, then. Things will have gotten interesting, won't they?"

CHAPTER FOUR

Despite the previous gloomy evening and the unusual atmosphere of the dour tavern, Wagner woke feeling refreshed and delighted to see the sun shining.

He stood at the cracked frame of the window in his small room, which overlooked the dirt road in front of the inn and the craggy mountains beyond the smooth pastures and untilled fields. The mountains looked lush in the morning glare, and his thoughts turned toward tramping in the nearby hills and tackling some of the distant peaks, once he was underway with his employment at the castle. He had climbed the snowy mountains of Bavaria and made a few climbing trips to Switzerland—once even successfully summiting the mighty Matterhorn. But those days had been before Britta and the grim hell that had followed her swift demise. Still, one of the things he hoped to do in his new life in the Carpathians was get his feet back in touch with the stone and soil of the mountains.

He threw the window open and breathed the cold air in deeply, then began his morning ritual of stretches and exercises. Afterward he cleaned himself and headed down to the tavern to break his fast. Even Miklos seemed chipper with the sun blazing brightly through the wide open door to the large room.

"Just one man to work on restoring a castle? Seems like quite a job, sir," Miklos said, while serving up a plate of sliced meats and chunky cheeses, dark mustards and steaming bread.

"I had discussed bringing on more men in my correspondence with the Count, once the project has begun," Wagner told him.

"More men?"

"And women." Wagner smiled.

"Women?" Miklos was stunned.

"Yes, my wife will join me in a few weeks, once I am settled."

Miklos's face had turned sour again and the man stalked off to the kitchen. Wagner figured the man was just perpetually ill-tempered, and the seeming joviality moments earlier was a fluke. He ate his food in silence, then returned to his room to pack his leather bags. When he came downstairs, he settled his bill with the waitress from the night before, who was manning the front counter. There was no sign of Miklos. She was pretty, as she pushed a handful of dark curls behind her ear, but no match for his wife. Still, he could see what would have attracted the local men to her. She had large brown eyes and long lashes. More importantly, her skin was clear and fine. This morning she wore a variation of the previous evening's dress, although the neckline was higher and she wore a scarf around her throat, tied in a small bow. Wagner assumed that as the night went on, she would remove the scarf, and the buttons holding the dress closed at the upper chest would slowly start to come undone. As the patrons got drunker, and spent more money, her attire would get more risqué. He had seen the same thing with Munich waitresses and bargirls. She certainly looked tired this morning, and squinted in the bright daylight flooding in through the tavern's few windows.

"Your coach is waiting for you, sir."

Wagner glanced at the waitress, then turned to the front of the tavern. He hadn't heard any coach approaching. He stepped into the open doorway and beheld a singular vehicle, unlike any coach he had seen.

It was deep black, and very tall and narrow. Wide enough, surely, for only one man—and not a very heavy man at that. The trim of the carriage was well-appointed with thick velvet drapes of a dark maroon in the windows. The horses at the lead were twin black stallions with luxuriant long bluish-black tails and shining silver head plates like armor. But their arrangement in the traces was bizarre—one of the two stallions was in front of the other.

The driver's seat was empty.

Wagner goggled at the strange carriage and wondered if it wouldn't simply tip over on a wide turn, never mind a sharp twist in a road.

"How very unique," he said.

Wagner looked around for the driver, but could see him nowhere.

Instead, he turned back toward the inn and found Miklos wearing an apron and holding his bags out for him. "Safe journey, sir."

"Thank you," Wagner took his cases and loaded them into the narrow carriage, then climbed into the seat and closed the door. He had had enough of the local hospitality. But Miklos lingered for just a moment outside the open window of the dark carriage.

"Herr Wagner," he said, drawing Wagner's eyes toward him. "I wouldn't bring your lady here. It's a very rough country."

Wagner was about to reply, but the carriage jolted into motion, throwing him back in his seat as the horses pulling the coach sped into a quick gallop. He slid forward on his seat, and then craned his neck out the open window to take in the driver.

The man seated in the driver's position was wearing a black cloak, and his head was hooded. Wagner could make out no features, other than that the man was very skinny, like the carriage, and must have stood close to six and a half feet tell when standing. He was hunched over into a dark crescent as he worked the reins, urging the horses faster. The noise from the stallions' hooves and the wheels of the carriage were such that Wagner made no attempt to converse with the driver—the man simply wouldn't hear him. Instead, he put his faith in the fact that any driver of the Count's would be extremely familiar with the road to the castle, no matter how dangerous it might be. Surely the coach driver's excellence could be counted upon.

Wagner sat back in the plush cushioned chair and watched the scenery roll by, as the verdant countryside blurred past. The rocking motion, combined with the exquisite fresh air, soon made him sleepy, and he found himself dozing lightly. When he woke from a jolt under the wheel of the carriage, he looked out the window and immediately realized why the carriage needed to be as narrow as it was: The road itself was narrow and gray as it wound through the tight mountain spaces, a precipitous drop just inches from the edge of the wheel. The height was dizzying, even for a mountaineer such as himself. Wagner was startled by the change in the landscape during his brief snooze, from green rolling alpine pastures to gray crumbling rock and jagged peaks. Even the weather had changed, from sunlit day to overcast leaded skies.

How long did I sleep?

And then he saw it.

Across a chasm of valley shrouded in mist and shadow, the structure loomed out of the morning, its natural base clouded by mists. The castle hunched upon the cliffs, its lone path twisting like a snake up the mountain. The rock around the structure was carved away by wind, and rain, and time, as if the castle itself was the last holdout against the ravages of a foul-tempered Mother Nature.

"Mein Gott. How did they even build that up there?"

It was exposed, like Neuschwanstein castle, back in Bavaria, yet even that glorious castle had more level ground around it. As far as Wagner could tell, the winding, narrow, stone bridge of land that led to the building was the only land still unaffected by the powers of nature. It was as if all the land had simply fallen away from the environs of the castle, leaving only the rectilinear edges and turreted roofline as evidence that a mighty mountain once stood around the structure.

To the untrained eye, the building appeared completely sound, but Andreas Wagner had worked with stone for most of his life, since apprenticing with his father. He could immediately spot areas that looked weak and others that looked as if they might have been subject to fire damage. Still, from this distance, he wouldn't be able to fully appraise the state of the building.

The carriage moved into a thick grove of evergreen trees, and his view of the massive castle was obstructed. The branches swiped at the carriage as it raced past at dizzying speed.

The road veered away from the view further, and the next few minutes were through dense alpine forest. Yet the driver showed no sign of slowing any time soon. The blur of nearby trees began to weary Wagner's eyes, so he shifted his view to the inside of the carriage, with its expensive upholstery.

When his next sight of the castle came, it was because the coach had burst from the forest onto the very edge of the narrow natural bridge to the Count's home. The building now loomed so large that he could not take in all of it through the tiny carriage window. Despite the disturbing plummet to either side of the vehicle, the driver still showed no signs of slowing the coach. They raced and clattered through a portcullis and into the main courtyard of the castle, with its bleak stone walls soaring up all around them. The driver finally halted the horses. It came so suddenly that Wagner thought they might crash into the wall of the main building. The complete lack of motion was disorienting after such heady speed. He could hear the stallions breathing hard and snorting at the head of the vehicle.

He stepped out of the coach onto the smooth stone flagstones of the courtyard. Once again, the driver had vacated his seat and had apparently moved quickly and silently out of sight. Wagner glanced at the courtyard from the gate. He looked up at the soaring height of the castle wall before him. Huge statues of ravens and old men with flowing beards and swords were scattered around the space. The ravens were

The castle hunched upon the cliffs, its lone path
twisting like a snake up the mountain.

massive—nearly six foot—and they were made of a stone of such a dark gray that it appeared black. Each statue of a man held a sword. *Most likely ancient Transylvanian war heroes, or perhaps prior owners of the castle*, Wagner thought. Either way, he found them intimidating in the courtyard, and he thought their arrangement very haphazard, as if the courtyard were at one time a sculptor's studio, and the pieces were wherever he felt like working that day.

Wagner turned his attention back to the castle. The door was a large slab of old heavy wood, with a thick iron band and supports, long since rusted. But what caught Wagner's eye immediately were the large rocks, some as large as a man's head, scattered around the courtyard as if dropped there. In fact, he knew they had been. He glanced up the immense front wall of the building to the towers and turrets and quickly located a few areas from where the chunks might have come. He would have his work cut out for him.

He moved to knock on the heavy door with his knuckles, when he found no bell or other way of announcing his presence. But before he could touch his flesh to the iron-banded door, it began to move. The door swung open, but no one stood on the other side to greet him.

CHAPTER FIVE

The door had swung inward silently, with no creak or groan. *At least the hinges are being oiled*, Wagner thought.

Although the upper reaches of the exterior of the castle were not well cared for, he saw that the more accessible areas indoors were well tended. Inside the door, the large hall had fine woodwork, and the walls were draped with old tapestries. The room was huge, and in similar castles Wagner had seen, the upper reaches were clogged with spider webs. But the inside of this room was immaculately clean—even the corners of the ceilings, far above his head.

A huge curving staircase dominated the room with a thick banister covered in hundreds of years of polish and wax. Doorways led off to other parts of the castle from this central entry foyer. A red Persian carpet covered the floor. At the edges of the enormous room, the black and white checked marble floor was visible. Windows high above on the front wall let in a stream of diffuse light, and Wagner noted that the sun, while it was shining through the clouds outside, did not directly pierce the windows. *They must be shaded to reduce glare*, he thought.

It the center of the room was a round wooden table with a vase of fresh flowers, and a thick envelope addressed "*My Dear Herr Wagner*" in a fine and curling script. Wagner stepped into the room and looked around. He was alone.

He moved to the table and opened the letter.

My Dear Herr Wagner,

I must humbly thank you for making the long and sometimes treacherous journey to my home from your distant Bavaria. As I am sure you must already have seen, the castle can benefit from the touch of a skilled craftsman such as yourself. It was sadly neglected for many years, and has, I am afraid, fallen into some disrepair.

It is with some regret that I must inform you I have been called away on business. I often travel long distances, and I am frequently away during the days. Do not let this concern you. I will make your acquaintance soon, and we will become close friends. My servant will prepare meals for you, and should you require any supplies, you will leave him a list at the breakfast table. He will be certain to secure the necessary items for you from the shops in the village.

You have the run of the castle for your inspections, and you may begin your work wherever you should see fit. Should you come across any portions of the buildings that are locked, this will be because they are very old and disused. I shall endeavor to locate the keys to these sections for you when I return. A room has been prepared for you, and I have included a small map of sorts indicating areas of the castle I know to require your stone-working services.

We shall meet soon. Until then, welcome.

D

Wagner looked up from the letter at the mention of a servant, but as far as he could determine, he was still alone in the cavernous room. He briefly inspected the parchment map, and then returned the letter and the map to the envelope from which they had come.

He thought it strange that the Count was not available to meet him, and that the servant was nowhere to be seen, either. He wondered whether the vanishing coach driver was the servant in question. He determined to settle into his room and then have a look around the castle, but it occurred to him that he had no idea where his room might be. The small hand-drawn map the Count had included indicated only areas of disrepair—most of which were near the upper reaches of the structure. There was no mention of where he would find his room, the kitchen, or the servant's quarters, for that matter.

"Right then," he said aloud. "I suppose the exploration will come first."

He strode across the lush carpet, examining the broad slabs of gray stone that made up the walls of the foyer. The foyer was in good shape, and he didn't think he would need to do any work in the large room; he knew from experience that the weaker sections would be the disused parts of the building. He crossed to a hallway that led toward the rear of the castle. Off the hall were doors to a small sitting room, a cramped space with a lovely antique writing desk, and a few rooms that were completely empty of furniture or decoration—they were little more than stone cells with bare walls, and they were oddly incongruent with the rest of the lushly decorated place. Wagner wondered whether the spaces were simply yet to be decorated, or if they had some other purpose. *For storage, perhaps?*

The thing he found most interesting were small nicks and cuts in the stone in various places along the walls and extending up high to the ceilings. The marks did not look natural, yet he could not fathom what purpose the original designers might have had for such marks and gouges in the stone.

At the end of the long limestone corridor with a seemingly new running carpet, he followed his nose to a large kitchen, with a wooden table, set for one. The room was awash with the glorious scents of warm, inviting food. There were two candles lit in the candelabrum on the table, as well as fine silver, a linen napkin, and what appeared to be Chinese porcelain, although Wagner was no expert. A large jug of water was dripping condensation onto the white lace tablecloth. A huge platter heaped with meat and cheese was the centerpiece, but he also found warm bread, mashed potatoes, and leafy green vegetables. There was probably enough food set out for five men or more, and most of it was still quite warm. Again, he glanced around, looking for the servant that might have prepared the meal. *He must have been here just moments ago.*

He was alone in the room, though, and not a pot or pan swung from the hanging rack as if it had been recently disturbed. Besides the food on the table, there was no indication that anyone had been in the room recently. Chopping surfaces were clean, and dishes were dry in the draining racks near the sink. Knives gleamed and were neatly arrayed on a preparation table. *Yet another mystery for another time*, he thought. He suddenly felt famished, and so, feeling quite guilty to be dining alone and at the effort of some unseen helper, he sat and ate.

Once again, as at the tavern, the food was fantastic. He was disappointed to be leaving so much of it behind. He did not know how many unseen servants the Count might have wandering around the sprawling castle, but it was very clear from the table's arrangement that this feast had been meant solely for him.

He stood from the table after eating and was about to retrace his steps back toward the front foyer, when he spotted a door ajar at the far corner of the kitchen. He strode across the room to the door. It was unlocked and revealed a descending spiral stone staircase. Thinking it might lead to the servant's quarters, and wishing to express his thanks for the fine meal, he began his descent.

CHAPTER SIX

The curving stairway was dark, but Wagner had snatched a candlestick from the kitchen before descending. The dull orange glow bounced and danced as he made his way deeper into the foundations of the castle. The stonework was good and solid, the limestone steps wide and smooth from years of foot traffic. The walls showed no signs of moisture, which was always a good thing. However, he found more of the strange nick marks in the walls a few feet up from the steps and going up to the stairwell's curved ceiling.

As he descended, he found room after room off the spiral steps, most of which were empty. Those that were not held items like crates and furniture covered in old dusty sheets. At first, Wagner was concerned with finding the servants, but the engineering part of his mind soon lost that thread, and he became completely engulfed in the mystery of what might lie at the bottom of the twisting stair, and why this stairwell and these rooms had been carved out of the rock. He was now far below the ground floor of the castle, and most likely far below any other basement levels of the structure as well. He pictured the castle like a giant pinwheel, with the staircase and its occasional small cramped rooms as the long stick.

How deep does this go?

When the stairs finally leveled out into an arched room, Wagner guessed the distance down from the kitchen to be some four hundred feet—an exceptionally long way to burrow into solid rock, only so you could place a room. He stepped into the arched room and instantly recognized it for what it was. A wine cellar. But the notion that someone would want a cellar this far below a castle boggled his mind. Surely there was something more.

The room, with its soaring arched ceiling, was filled with hundreds of wooden wine racks, each filled with dusty bottles. The arrangement of the racks was like a maze, but Wagner easily navigated through them. Since childhood, he had always had an innate ability to keep track of his location in busy markets or twisting alleyways. As he had grown older, he found the ability extended to not getting lost in the forests, where his friends would be clueless as to their direction. He moved around the room, the dank air suggesting that this far down into the mountain, water had done its work and found the tiny cracks and crevices it always does. At the edges of the room, he found the walls were oddly shaped nooks, coves, and crannies that allowed wooden racks to be placed at all angles to hold the cellar's voluminous collection of dusty wine bottles. Wagner did not know wines, but he had seen a few large collections of which the owners were proud. This one would have made all those men seem like amateurs.

He stepped into one corner, the light from his candle flickering and casting huge shadows up the racks of bottles. But the shadows did not hold his attention. Again, the architecture was what took root in his mind. With his many years of working with stone and buildings, his well-trained eyes could not help but notice the finer details of his surroundings: The twisting bends and corners, nooks, and even crawlspaces of the place were incongruent with a simple wine cellar—even a spectacularly large one such as this—and he wondered whether the maze-like design had been intentional. He could see the stone walls behind the racks contributed to the overall design. It was not just the rack arrangement, though, it was something else, something he could not put a finger on. Perhaps the quality of the stone differed? Was it a stone much harder, and thus more difficult to cut? Or maybe the room had been fashioned from a naturally occurring cavern in the mountain? The other possibility—that the room had intentionally been designed with a maze-like quality, to confound and delay those moving through it—seemed absurd. That was something that belonged more on a battlefield, not in a damp wine cellar. He tried to examine the stone through the spaces in the wooden racks, but his feeble candlelight and the smoothness of the stone made it difficult to determine the material. *Probably local limestone, but why would someone polish the stone down here?*

Then he found the door.

Other than the access to the spiral stair, the door at the far back of the cellar was the only other egress. But the wide wooden door was locked, and Wagner did not have a key. He spent a moment looking at the wall where the door sat obstinately taunting him. He examined the frame of the door, the floor, and the corners of the wall. *Yet another mystery, for yet another day. This place will be fun.*

Then he turned and strolled across the floor to the doorway to the stairs. He began his ascent, and he whistled as he climbed. As an alpinist that had climbed in Bavaria and the Swiss Alps, a long trudge up a spiral stair held little difficulty for him, and he was excited to explore the rest of this strange castle.

When the curious German was gone, one of the racks of wine bottles swung silently away from a wall, like a hinged door. The bottles themselves were so snug in their wooden beds within the rack that no glass tinkled from the movement. The hinges on the rack were well oiled and moved in absolute silence. Behind the rack, an open stone doorway revealed a large room with a bed and several grated holes in the floor. The man that had been quietly standing in the room and watching Wagner stepped out. He closed the gliding wine rack façade and moved further into the gloom of the darkened cellar.

He had no need of candlelight to see. He was used to the dark. Life with the Master had given him certain gifts and opportunities, while at the same time taking away so much more. He knew the Master had hired the German to come restore some of the stonework around the castle. He had been expecting the man. Still, he was surprised the stonemason had found his way down to the wine cellar so quickly. The man had watched through the rows of dusty green bottles, while the stonemason puzzled over the door to the Master's private room. He wondered how much the German might suspect. Impossible to tell. He knew only that it was his duty to protect the Master.

The German was tall and thin. His hair was a shaggy blonde mane that fell to the shoulders of his collar. He had looked harmless enough until he began scrutinizing the wall of the Master's lair, as if he were considering how best to knock it down with a sledgehammer. But then he had left, defeated by the simple lock on the door, whistling his way up the stairs as if he had no cares in the world.

The man moved from the wine rack to the foot of the stairs and strained his ears. He could just barely hear the stonemason, far above him up the twisting steps. Too cheery. The German did not belong. *I will have to do something about it.* He started up the stairs, thinking about how he might kill the German and make it look like an accident. *The Master need never know.*

CHAPTER SEVEN

When dusk finally came, he would awake from his long slumber. The servant waited just outside the room for him, in the dark. The Master would wake quickly each time, stepping from his place of rest with nimble agility, and moving rapidly to the door. The servant would always greet him. It had been this way each day, for years.

The servant longed for these interactions with the Master. Most days, he would perform his duties around the castle as rapidly as he could, so that he might spend more time waiting, just outside the door to the Master's chambers. Today had been different because of the presence of the nosy German. The servant had followed the German intruder unseen throughout the day. The servant understood why the stonemason had been invited to the castle, but he instantly disliked the man. He also hated to wait on the man, always making sure to include some of his saliva in the warm food he prepared for the German.

But thoughts of the German quickly faded as the servant checked his fob watch and saw the time. Even in the dark of the cellar, with no windows nearby and no sources of light, he could tell when dusk was upon him. He did not really need the watch. He always knew when the Master would wake.

He reached out for the latch to the door with one hand, the key in the other. He was about to slip the key into its cold metal lockplate when he heard the presence on the other side of the door. The lock tumbled of its own accord. The servant stepped back and held his breath, prepared to behold his beloved Master.

A gust of wind blew the door wide, and it slammed against the hard stone wall. The servant dropped to his knees, as he had done so many times. He hardly noticed the rough surface anymore through the calluses skin on his bony legs.

"Master," he whispered.

The Master stood and glared, his deep eyes like twin pools of lava tumbling through a black void. He looked down and the servant for a moment, then gently waved his hand, indicating that the servant should rise.

As he stood, almost a head taller than the Master, the servant was eager for a command, but more than that, he longed for the Master to fulfill his promise. A promise of immortality.

"Tell me," the Master said. His voice was like a smooth scraping of fabric over rough stone. His eyes were devastating, even in the darkness. The servant would not meet those eyes. Not if he could help it.

Looking at the floor, the servant stepped back to allow his Master to walk first through the maze of wine racks. "The German has come, my Master. He has fed and explored the castle, before he settled in to his room on the west side. I put him on the second floor."

The Master swept through the darkened cellar with no difficulty—the pattern of the racks was known to him, and he had no need for light to see. "Fine," he told the servant. He paused at the door to the spiral stair that would lead him up and out. Into the night.

"Is there anything else?" his Master asked. There was a hint of menace in his voice. The servant understood that somehow, the Master knew there was more. He always knew. It was useless to try to hide something from him.

"The German found the door to your chambers," the servant said. He took a quick step back against the wall of dusty wine bottles behind him, in case he had displeased the Master. Not that it would have made any difference. The retreat was instinctual. "He studied the door before departing. I do not like him. Will you kill him?"

The Master turned his eyes—embers now catching into brilliant flame—onto the servant. The servant felt his head being raised, his chin lifted by an unseen force, until his eyes met those of the Master. He wanted to whimper and cry, but he knew that would do no good.

The Master was silent for seconds, but it felt like minutes to the nervous servant. "He is a mason, Petran. He is interested in stone. He is also my guest. I must afford him every courtesy."

The Master turned his eyes back to the doorway into the spiral stair, and Petran felt the power that had grasped his face in the darkness release its hold. He lowered his eyes to the floor again, grateful for the reprieve from his Master's terrible wrath, but sullen about the verdict on the German.

"All the same, Petran," the Master began to ascend the stairs, a slow and measured step at a time. "Let us see if we can dissuade the man from returning to the cellar for awhile. You will ensure that the door at the top of the stairs remains locked. And you will watch him."

"Yes, Master." Petran dipped his head under the doorframe and followed his Master up the steps. It was always the same. The Master woke ravenously hungry, but he would take the first fifty or so steps at a leisurely pace, before his hunger aroused in him a greater need. Then he would flee up the stairs with abandon, seeking his first meal of the night. Petran would dutifully follow up the steps, until he was left behind.

"I hunger, Petran. Where shall I go tonight?" The Master's voice was still calm, the embrace of his need not yet fully upon him. He would remain civil and restrained until it had him in its grip. Petran had seen it countless times. How he longed to know that need. To feel that power.

"There is a lovely new serving girl at the tavern. She is young."

"I know. I have…seen her already," the Master stopped on the steps to remove his shoes. Petran waited, then reached out his hand to receive the black leather shoes. The Master stretched his arms and his back. He did not turn to face Petran. "Do not wait up for me, Petran. I need you rested in the morning, to keep an eye on the German."

With that, the Master reached out his hands to one wall on the side of the stairwell. He stepped up on to the wall with his toes finding purchase in crevices too small for Petran to see. Then, crawling like a spider, the Master worked his way up the wall toward the ceiling of the ascending passageway. In a blur, he was gone up the stairs. A creature of habit. Always the same. When the Master needed to run, he preferred the high places.

CHAPTER EIGHT

A week passed before Wagner met the Count.

There was much to do during that time. Wagner had wandered the dark halls and the crevices of most parts of the vast castle to which he had access. Some of the parts of the castle were still locked, and he had made a careful note of those sections on the map the absentee Count had left for him. Others were inaccessible from fallen rubble and burnt or splintered timber. He came to the conclusion that the castle had suffered from a fire at some point in the last thirty years, and entire portions of the castle appeared to have been abandoned as a result. Black scorch marks were still visible in some places on the gray stone walls, and more than once he had encountered a pile of debris so high that it almost resembled an intentional barricade.

Still, he was determined to survey the extent of the damage to the structure, and he had even gone so far as to explore the base of the building along the cliffs, utilizing rope—and in one case on the northwest corner, going so far as to employ his alpine abilities with hammer and pitons. The damage was mostly superficial. The building had stood for hundreds of years and would continue to do so. Wagner made extensive notes and diagrams for areas requiring work, whether the need was minor or major.

In the week of exploration, he still did not encounter a single servant in the castle, yet his meals were always laid on the table three times a day. His room was cleaned as well. By the fourth day, with no sign of the Count or his helpers, Wagner began to plan a way to spy the servant setting out his meals. He rose two hours earlier and made his way to the large kitchen, with the intent of spotting the servant laying out the morning meal. But when he arrived in the kitchen, his place at the table had already been set. He finished the food and left the kitchen, then unexpectedly came back twenty minutes later, hoping to find the servant clearing the dishes, but the dishes were still in place on the table. When he went away and came back in another twenty minutes, the table had been cleared, and the dishes washed.

He gave up his espionage and resumed his explorations of the castle and his inspection of cracks and joints for a few hours. He lost track of time—he had intended to again attempt to catch out the servant at lunch—and by the time he made it back to the kitchen, his stomach growling for a snack, the table had been secretly prepared again.

On the sixth day he left a note on the table, thanking the invisible servant for the meals, and inviting the person to remain behind, so he might speak to him or her and ask questions about the nature of the damage to the building. He also left a short list of needed supplies, both personal and professional.

On the morning of the seventh day, his meal was set at the table again, as usual. There was no sign of any servant, but the items he had requested—a blank journal, a pen, washing soap, a small hand trowel, a larger shovel, and a pick ax—were all either on the table or leaning against it. He inspected the assembled tools. They were crude, but they would work to help him clear rubble and dig away any crumbling bits of mortar, so he could see just how far certain cracks on the third floor went.

He still had the upper reaches of the castle to explore and document on his Map of Improvements, as he came to think of it. And, of course, there was the thing he had discovered yesterday before hunger drove him down to dinner and then to sleep. It weighed on his mind, and he yearned to investigate it.

Right. Everyone needs to take a day of rest, he told himself.

Wagner returned first to his spacious room with the tools, and left them on a dressing table. He collected a small leather backpack he had brought with him from Germany, and he placed the leather-bound journal and the fountain pen inside it. Then he went to one of his larger valises, a rectangular black case, and retrieved one of his most prized possessions. The tan paper tube was about a foot long, with shiny brass rings capping either end. One of the brass caps held a bulbous convex glass. The all-new, American, "electric device" would allow him to see in the dark in brief flashes, but the filament and the zinc-carbon batteries would need to be shut off and rested often. Still, this tool, given to him by his policeman uncle in New York, would be just the thing for his explorations today. The tube, carefully packed in its velvet-lined wooden box, went into the small leather backpack, and he set off.

He mounted the narrow stairs to the third floor of the castle with an enthusiasm he had been lacking in his previous exploits. On those days, he had been working, mapping, and analyzing damage. Today, he would be indulging his hobby. So when he reached the corridor off the wooden stairs that led to the darkened third floor hall, with its dreary stone walls and lack of windows, Wagner was not put off. He moved into the gloom away from the stairs, and waited until he could no longer see in the darkness, before he lit a match to get a glimpse of his surroundings. He had previously explored some of this hallway, and he remembered the double doors of banded wood that led to his destination. He would save the American device for later, when it would be more useful. For now, the flickering orange flame from his wooden match threw off all the wavering light he needed. He proceeded down the maroon Oriental rug that lined the long corridor until he reached the double doors. Outside the doorway was a black iron sconce with the three candles he had placed the day before. He lit them just as the match began to gutter. The first two candles caught, but the third did not. Still, the light from the two red wax sticks illuminated the hallway before the wooden match died. He raised one of the candles, careful not to allow any wax droplets to fall onto the carpet. He lit the third candle in the sconce and replaced the first stick in its place.

His hands now free, he moved to the double doors and swung them both inward, then inhaled the smell and smiled. The distinctive odor of a library swept over him, filling him with memories of his childhood. Paper. Dust. Glue. Leather. Some mildew, although he would not know the extent of the damaged volumes until he had taken an inventory of the place. He stepped into the blackness and stopped to squat on the floor. He removed his pack and the wooden box. Now was the time for the "flashlight," as people were coming to call the American electric device. He would only be able to use it in short bursts, but it would be enough for him to determine whether it would be safe to bring some of the candlesticks in and light sconces or candelabra. He would not risk setting an entire library aflame.

The blaze of yellow light from the carbon-filament device showed a massive room with what Wagner guessed must have been at least twenty-thousand volumes, all carefully resting on beautifully carved wooden shelving that lined the walls and ran up into one of the castle's towers for at least three further floors. Delicate wrought iron spiral stairs led up into the upper reaches of darkness. Wagner caught his breath and shut off the tube. "Mein Gott!"

The floor appeared, in his quick glance with the electric light, to be all white marble and was clear of papers or books, so he now had no fear of using the candles. He stepped back out of the room and pulled a bare candlestick from the sconce on the wall, and then re-entered the room with it. The glow of the flame lent a far warmer feeling to the already magical room than the harsh electric light had. Wagner did not know if he had ever seen so many books in a personal library. It was like one of the great university libraries in Germany, the stacks seemingly endless. He turned to the wall just inside the doors and found more sconces with older yellow wax candles already in place. He lit all eight sticks before turning to again appreciate the room.

The sconces threw off a greater illumination than his electric tube had, and now he could see the rooms off to the side of the main foyer, the balconies of the upper levels, and the twisting turning shelves at the far end of the room. He was reminded of the wine cellar, with its peculiar maze-like design.

As he scanned the dim recesses of the cavernous library, Andreas Wagner thought he might be in heaven. A lover of reading since he was a boy in lederhosen, he would devour anything with a binding, whether a story or an instruction manual. He had known upon taking the job in Hungary that it might take him months, or even years, to finish his work, depending on the structural damage to the castle. He had been prepared mentally for a long stretch of no access to reading, due to the castle's remote location. But now, seeing the Count's immense personal library, Wagner wondered if it might be in his best interest to exaggerate the time it would take to complete the restoration work on the building. He could spend his entire life in this library and not read even half of the volumes it contained.

Too honest to consider such a thought for long, he dismissed it and ventured further into the depths of the library, lighting candles where he found them, and scanning the golden lettering on the spines of the thick leather-bound books. In moments, he was lost, both physically in the labyrinth of the place, and mentally in a blissful world of the written word.

Dusk came without notice. Wagner had occasionally gnawed on a small loaf of bread and a larger hunk of cheese he had brought with him in his pack, but for the most part, the day passed without his realizing it.

The books were all.

He sat in a plush leather armchair he had found on the fourth floor of the library—*four floors!*—and rested his feet against the nearby railing. He was well into a serial story in the thousandth issue of Blackwood's Magazine, by a fellow he had never heard of before. Conrad. *Heart of Darkness*. He was about to absentmindedly turn yet another page, when he heard a shuffling noise from below him in the depths of the library.

Wagner set the magazine aside reluctantly. The story had been engaging, and he had been pleasantly surprised to find how up-to-date the Count's library was on modern popular fiction. He stood slowly, feeling stiffness from having sat still so long. He leaned over the railing to glance down to the marble floor, where he had heard the sound. Surely this was his much sought after servant, and the railing four floors up would provide him the perfect spying vantage.

Instead of finding the scurrying servant though, what he found four floors below him was far more disconcerting.

The lowest level of the library was plunged into blackness. The candles on the walls on that level and out in the corridor had died. He quickly checked the time on his fob watch—a battered, brass thing he had found in a small shop in Switzerland—and saw that it was evening, but not so late the candles would have run down to the quicks on their own. *The servant must have extinguished them.*

Wagner picked up the tubular flashlight and the box of matches he had set on the small table by the plush chair. He moved to go to the end of the balcony and descend the spiral stairs. He would just have to re-light the candles. Otherwise finding his way out of the room once he had returned his reading stack to the shelves might prove tricky.

He heard the shuffling noise once again, but this time it came from up on the fourth level, with him. The opposite direction this time, down at the other end of the long balcony, in a part of the level he had yet to explore, and which was still dark. He turned toward the sound, and when he saw a flicker in his peripheral vision, he turned back toward the stairs. The candle by the stairwell had gone out now as well. Only the candle on the small table next to his reading chair remained lit.

The rest of the library was cloaked in darkness, and Wagner felt suddenly that only his island of comforting ocher light was safe. Chastising himself for acting like a child, he stepped forward, passing the lone candle, and making for the unexplored part of the fourth floor.

He had taken only a few steps past his little reading nook when a sharp gust of wind blew past him, mussing his hair, making his unbuttoned vest flap open, and extinguishing the last of his light.

Then the shuffling sound began again in the dark.

He was initially seized with a paralyzing terror, but then as the smoke from the extinguished candle wafted past his nose, filling him with the familiar burnt scent, he once again calmed and berated himself.

A window must be open, he thought.

He recalled the layout of the next several feet along the railing on the balcony; he had been up here for hours. He moved forward in the dark without resorting to the matches or his electric light. When he heard the shuffling again, he worried for the books. *Could be rats. Possibly in the walls. They will eat the bindings. I must set some traps tomorrow.*

But the noise did not sound like the skittering feet of rats. Wagner had seen and heard plenty of them in Germany. This noise was soft but persistent. Like the beat of a bird's wings or like a dog continuously licking its chops.

As he stepped into the area at the end of the balcony, where his reading light had not penetrated all afternoon, he stopped and listened hard in the complete darkness.

Nothing. The fluttering sound had vanished.

Wagner raised the electric tube in the blackness in front of him and pressed the ignition lever.

The room strobed into focus with an excruciating white brilliance, like a flash of lightning. Before him stood a creature, almost like a man, but with a mouth full of teeth like a wolf. Its eyes were red burning coals. The thing was in obvious pain and anguish from the light, recoiling in horror, as its image—*black, so much blackness, as if the shadows had retreated to the thing and wrapped around it like a cloak*—terrified Wagner. His finger slipped off the lever and the room was immediately swallowed by darkness.

When he managed, with shaking hands, to ignite the flashlight again, he found he was once again alone in the room, with nothing more than shelves, books, and the fleeting image of the creature in his mind's eye.

And then, from behind him, came the clearing of a throat.

"You must be Stonemaster Andreas Wagner," a voice as smooth as velvet said. "I am Count Dracula."

Wagner whipped around with the beam of light from the electric device. He was surprised to find a man at the far end of the balcony, by the stairs. He could have sworn the voice was right behind him.

The man was about the same height as Wagner, wearing a long traveling coat, vest, and scarf. He was young—or at least younger than Wagner had expected. In their correspondence, the Count had seemed an older man. But the man that stood before him could not have been more than thirty-five years of age.

The Count stood solemnly by the vast bookshelves, his countenance one part amusement and the other part disdain. His hair was long and dark, one strand of it falling across his brow. His eyes were a deep dark color, and Wagner felt like they were drilling into his soul. But then the man smiled widely, showing his perfectly ordinary and white teeth. It was a friendly and inviting smile, and Wagner was instantly put at ease. *That could not have been this man, could it? His teeth! Was I just seeing things?* He momentarily discarded the image of the creature he had glimpsed, and recalled his manners.

"Count. I hope you do not mind my exploring your wonderful library," Wagner said as he strode down the balcony and relit the candle on his reading table before extinguishing his flashlight and returning it to its box. He then turned to shake the Count's extended hand.

"Not at all," replied the Count. "I am delighted to meet you and to discover that, like me, you are also a bibliophile. The best gentlemen are." The man smiled warmly as they shook hands, and Wagner noted that while the handshake was firm, the skin of the Count's hand was cool to the touch and as smooth as fine marble.

"I was beginning to think we might never meet," Wagner began as their embrace broke.

"I must apologize, sir. My work, at times, takes me far afield. Have you had time to familiarize yourself with the castle?" Wagner noted that the Count spoke with some formality, but his manner was very familiar.

"I have, sir. The damage is extensive in some places, but most of it is superficial. I don't anticipate any problems with the work, but I will need to bring on an assistant, as we had discussed."

"Of course, of course." The Count glanced at Wagner's reading stack, picking up items and smiling as he returned them to the table. "You have good taste. You still intend to hire this man, Bischoff?"

"Yes, sir. Fridtjof Bischoff—Fritz—is a first-class stone worker and a good friend. I've asked him to come with my wife. He will be bringing his own wife, Gretchen, so the ladies will have each other for company, as we men get to the work." Wagner felt uncomfortable lying about Gretchen being married to Fritz, but he had discussed the story with them ahead of time, suggesting it would be less likely to cause a stir.

The Count paused in his examination of the reading stack and slowly turned to Wagner. His face was suddenly serious.

The count stood solemnly by the vast book shelves,
his countenance one part amusement and the other part disdain.

"That…is probably a very good idea, Mr. Wagner." He smiled widely again, and his teeth glittered in the yellow light.

"I may yet again be called away on business," the Count said, as he began walking back toward the stairs. Wagner followed him. "I trust all your needs are being taken care of?"

"I have yet to actually see one of your servants, Count, but they have been very helpful in providing my meals and procuring my tools for me."

"Ah. Petran is shy sometimes. I am sure you will see him around at some point." The Count turned and abruptly strode to the top of the stairs. Wagner followed him, and when the Count reached the steps he turned again.

"I must take my leave of you, my good Andreas, for I am quite tired from this recent excursion to Serbia." They shook hands again.

"Of course, sir," Wagner replied. "I hope your trip was a successful one. What kind of work is it that you do?"

The Count smiled broadly again. "I am an expert on rare disorders of the blood."

"Oh! A doctor, then?" Wagner smiled back.

"No. For me it is purely a personal interest and one of research. I am called upon to examine many individuals, though. Have a good night sir, and enjoy the rest of your reading." With that, the Count turned rapidly, his coat swirling around him. Wagner was briefly reminded of the thing he thought he had seen—*The shadows! The fangs!*—before he dismissed the vision as pure nerves. As the Count descended the spiral stair into darkness, Wagner returned to his reading stack and determined to return his selections to the shelves before bed, with the exception of the Conrad, which he would take with him to his room. When he reached his small table with his belongings, the lower levels of the library began to glow again.

He stepped over to the rail and looked down to see the Count now on the lower level and crossing the marble floor. *How did he get down so fast?* The man walked along the wall, past the already re-lit candlesticks on each sconce. Wagner watched with amazement, as with each candle the Count passed, the small lick of flame would first practically gutter, and then, once the Count had passed the sconce, its flame would surge again into full brightness. Before his mind could comprehend what he had just seen, the Count had left the room, his feet appearing to glide over the floor more than walk.

My mind is definitely playing tricks on me.

CHAPTER NINE

Wagner saw the Count only in passing during the following days. He hardly gave any thought to the hideous apparition that had appeared before him in the gloom of the library. His rational mind, in the light of day, assumed he had been dozing in the chair. The whole sequence of the events was now muddled in his mind.

Instead of dwelling on it, he had set to work the following day, hauling rubble in a rickety wheelbarrow and dumping what portions he saw no further use for over the edge of the castle's cliffs. He was thrifty, though, and carefully assessed each stone or piece of jagged timber for its potential of being reused, when it came time for shoring up walls or fixing damage. The work kept him busy from his breakfast until his dinner. He would take a brief break for lunch, but he often found himself taking his sandwich with him and consuming it quickly on the way back to the wheelbarrow. The ability to lose himself in his work took his mind off the tragic events of the past.

At the end of the fourth day after meeting the Count in the library, Wagner entered the kitchen expecting to find his dinner, but instead an empty table and a single lit candle awaited him. On the table, a small handwritten note rested in the place where he normally ate.

The Count requests your presence at an informal dinner in the parlor, off the library.
—Petran

Wagner looked at the note briefly, then turned to head up to the library. He was not sure of the location of any room that might be called a 'parlor' near the library, but he felt confident he could find the Count, wherever the man might be. He went by his room and collected his small notebook and pen, thinking the Count might have some specific instructions for him, and then proceeded to make his way to the library. The corridor outside the double doors was dark, but inside the library there was a small flickering light. As Wagner stepped into the entrance to the library, he saw the source of the light was coming from a door on the wall to his left. He had missed the door on his last visit to the library, enchanted as he had been with the books. His journey had taken him deeper into the stacks off to the right, and eventually into the upper levels and balconies.

Now he stepped into the doorway off the library and took in the rich upholstery and fine drapes of the room. The carpet was thick and lush. Some dimly lit oil paintings adorned the walls, along with more of the sorts of tapestries he had seen in the corridors and in the castle's lobby. At the far wall, a curtain had been pulled part way across the wall. He realized it obscured an entryway to another room. A wide arch that, with the curtain pulled, would appear to be a wall, but was in fact a room divider. The source of the candlelight was on the other side of the curtain. He took a few steps through the small sitting room toward the curtain, but stopped. He heard a curious slurping noise from the other side of the curtain.

Suddenly, he felt he should announce his presence.

"Count? It is I, Herr Wagner."

A swift shuffling noise came from beyond the curtain. Then he heard a sound he recognized. That of a man standing up from an old chair.

"Ah, Herr Wagner," came the smooth voice. "Do join me."

The Count pulled the curtain aside with a flourish, revealing an identical sitting room on the other side. The same rich burgundy fabrics had been used on its walls. The carpet was all of one piece with the first sitting room. It had clearly been cut to fit the space from wall to wall. More faded tapestries and oil paintings with gilded ornate wooden frames decorated the walls, while plush settees and chairs filled the floor space of the room.

The Count stepped back into the room and returned to the chair in which he had been seated, a small bowl of dark soup rested on a table next to his chair. He also had a crystal goblet of deep red wine on the table. Wagner noted that it was nearly empty. He worried briefly that he might be late—the Count had clearly started without him.

"Please, sit," the Count encouraged him. Wagner noted another small table with a wine glass and a bowl of steaming soup for him. Based on how much steam the soup gave off, it could not have been in the room more than a few minutes. *Perhaps I am not late after all.*

"I hope you will forgive me for beginning without you, but I was famished. I've just returned from a long day up north." The Count smiled a small tight smile, then set back in his chair as if he was finished with his meal. Although the wine glass was nearly empty, the man's bowl was practically full.

"Of course, Count. Thank you so much for inviting me to dinner." Wagner was starving, and he hoped there would be more than just the soup. The normal meals Petran served him were huge. By comparison, the soup was just a snack. Despite his hunger, he felt a compulsion to wait for the Count's encouragement that he should eat. "I have been hard at work these past few days. I would relish some conversation."

"Yes, of course," the Count told him. "Petran informs me that you have been working very diligently, often not even taking time for a proper lunch. I can assure you that you are under no time constraints to finish your work, my good sir. Please, eat. While your soup is still warm." The Count gestured slightly with his hand to the bowl, and Wagner was surprised at the length of the man's fingernails. Wagner picked up his spoon and sampled the thick soup. It was too hot, but he made a show of enjoying the mostly bland, but slightly meaty, taste.

The Count took up his wine goblet and leaned far back into his chair. The sole candle in the room left the man mostly in shadow. He slowly sipped from the rim of the glass, his eyes never leaving Wagner.

Wagner ate a few spoonfuls of the soup, waiting for the Count to initiate the conversation. He wasn't quite sure what the Count wanted to discuss with him. He assumed the man would want to talk about the restoration of the castle, or maybe their shared tastes in reading. But the Count remained silent and his gaze never wavered. The look was beginning to make Wagner uneasy.

"Are you well, Count?" Wagner asked, after a few moments.

As if coming out of a slight dream, the Count sat forward in his chair. "I am sorry. Forgive me, I was lost in memory. You were saying?" The man's demeanor seemed like that of an old and fragile grandfather coming out of a cloud of recollection. Wagner was again struck by the odd contrast in the man's bearing and his looks. He appeared to be a young man—possibly younger than Wagner. He wondered at the memory that had so absorbed the Count, but knew it would be rude to ask.

"I was wondering if you wanted to hear about the restoration work," Wagner said, for lack of a better conversation topic.

"I am certain you have things well in hand. Do you have all that you require?" The Count leaned back into the shadow of his wingback chair once again.

"Actually, you had said in your welcome letter that you would obtain the keys for me to those upper rooms in the east wing that are locked." The Count raised an eyebrow and held his gaze on Wagner. He looked as if he remembered no such promise.

"To the rooms beyond the debris pile?" Wagner pressed. "I believe the worst of the structural damage would be up there, and I—"

"Of course," the Count interrupted him. "Petran will ensure the keys are left for you at the breakfast table. I do not wish to impede your efforts in any way. You find your task manageable, then?"

"Yes. What I have seen so far confirms my initial assessment, that there will be a few areas that require intense reconstruction, and some things will be slowed by the onset of winter, but I do not anticipate the project to take longer than we had discussed in our correspondence." Wagner felt in his element at last, speaking about the repairs he would effect to the stone. They spoke for another twenty minutes on the subject, when the Count once again cut him off.

"I apologize again, but I must take my rest. I have an early start in the morning, for yet another trip. Perhaps we might dine again, on a different day. I would like to speak with you of your favorite authors, and of the latest books in Germany. It has been some time since I have traveled there."

"Of course." Wagner stood. "I shall look forward to it."

The Count stood as well and left the room swiftly, as if he were late for an appointment. Wagner looked after the man. *He is an odd sort*, he thought. *One moment sounding older than his years, and at other times seemingly young and vigorous.*

Wagner returned to his chair and sat down to finish his wine. He liked the taste of it. He didn't know much about wines, but the flavor rolled around and under his tongue. He was feeling warm and tired as he sat back in his chair, now looking at the empty chair across from him. The Count's bowl remained on the table untouched. The crystal goblet with the wine was gone. Had the Count taken it with him? Wagner couldn't recall. Suddenly the long day and the warm soup in his belly combined to throw a comfortable blanket of sleepiness over him. He fought for just an instant to stay awake, but then embraced the sensation and fell to dozing in his chair.

CHAPTER TEN

Wagner woke deep in the night thinking he had heard a scream, but was unable to recall his dreams. In a moment, his head cleared, and with no further sound in the room save his own breathing, he realized he was only half awake. Any sounds he had heard were from his own sleep-addled mind. The candle in the parlor had burned down to a molten lump of wax, the flame in the last throes of its life. Wagner blew out the candle promptly made his way to his room, extinguishing other lit candles in their sconces as he went, and fell into his bed.

The following day he found a thick ring of brass keys on the breakfast table. He continued his work around the castle, and eventually found a few dust-choked rooms close to the top of the castle, where the entire roof had caved in. He understood instantly why those sections had been closed off. A few days later he was hauling yet another load down the makeshift plank ramp he had fashioned to get from the second story down the main stairs to the echoing foyer, when it occurred to him that since he had been given the keys to the locked doors of the structure, he hadn't yet made the descent down to the wine cellar again, to inspect its locked room. He recalled both the dank smell of the cellar and the thought that he'd had about potential water damage.

I really should give it a further look.

Although he had still not met Petran, the table was always set for him three times a day, and as he left lists of things he needed, he would always find those items in the kitchen at mealtimes. Instead of taking his wheelbarrow load out to the courtyard to dump, he left it standing in the foyer, setting the rear metal legs down carefully, so as not to scuff the checked marble floor.

He walked to the kitchen, keeping an eye out for Petran, but as usual, the room was vacant. He crossed the room for the cellar door and curiously found it locked. He took out the large ring of keys that had been left for him, and he tried a few keys in the door until he felt one satisfyingly seat itself in the lock. He twisted, and with a loud clunking, the lock tumbled, and the door opened.

Many areas of the castle were perpetually dark, because of its poor number of windows. Those that were present were often shaded by architectural design, almost as if this part of Hungary had once been afflicted with blistering desert-like sunshine, instead of the cold, drizzly, and foggy days Wagner had experienced since his arrival. Due to the gloom, he had taken to always traveling the building's maze of corridors and abundance of rooms armed with his small leather backpack, which contained his flashlight as well as several candles and matches. He took out one of the small sticks now and lit it for his descent of the spiral stairs.

Along the descent, he popped his head into each of the rooms again, noting that nothing about them had changed. He found it interesting that the last time the door had been ajar, and this time it was locked, yet no one seemed to be using anything in any of the rooms. Wagner wondered if perhaps Petran had been getting into the wines while the Count had been away, and now that the man had returned, Petran was wisely keeping the stairs to the cellar locked.

None of my business.

When Wagner reached the twisty cellar, he went directly to the door on the far wall. He set his candle down on the floor, in a small dish he carried in his pack. Then he moved to the lock and began to try his clunky keys. The ring held twenty-eight of the long brass keys, each for different parts of the castle. The Count had told him the skeleton master key for all of the locks had been missing for generations.

Wagner made a methodical search, having placed a small bit of red string around the barrel of one of the keys, so he wouldn't lose track of those keys he had tried. The tactic had worked well for him when trying the other locked doors in the building. He had yet to not find the correct key.

When he tried the last key against this lock to no avail, he frowned. Had he miscounted? He tried each key a second time, beginning with the key with the string, and carefully moving one key at a time around the ring.

None of the keys worked on this door.

He took a step back and looked again at the frustrating door—its hinges were on the other side—and frowned again. He could smell a deep odor of rot and decay, and the smell was stronger nearer the door. He would have to get in there to determine the extent of the damage. Any structural problems this low into the mountain probably would not affect the stability of the rest of the castle, but Wagner was not one to leave such things to chance.

"What are you doing?" a voice hissed at him in English from the shadows.

Wagner was startled and dropped the ring of keys, as he spun around.

The sound the brass keys made, clattering and skittering across the stone floor, made the man cringe, as if it caused him acute pain. He stood before Wagner, but well above him. The man must have been seven feet tall. He was painfully thin and gangly, although his form was somewhat masked by his well-tailored dark suit. His hair was long over his brow, and greasy, as if it had not been washed in weeks. In the flickering light of the candle, the man's eyes looked black.

"Oh, you gave me quite a start," Wagner said.

"What are you doing?" the man repeated. He seemed to be barely containing his anger.

"My name is Andreas Wagner. The Count has hired me to do renovations on the castle."

The man sneered.

"I know who you are," he said. "What are you doing *here*?"

Wagner raised an eyebrow at the man, then bent to collect the keys from the floor. When he stood again, he stared directly into the tall man's eyes. "I was looking for the key to this room. Are you Petran?"

The man's expression changed in the dim light. Wagner could almost see him deciding to check his hostility. "I am Petran. The key to that room has been lost for many years. You do not need to go in there."

"Oh, but I must. There's a smell of rot. There could be damage to the foundation—"

"You do not need to go in there," Petran said again, firmly. "It is only an old root cellar, and was never used, even when we had the key."

"I see," Wagner said, collecting his candle. But he felt there was more to it. Besides being snide, Petran was protecting something. Perhaps he had been lifting bottles from the Count's wine collection after all, and storing them in the root cellar. Although Wagner was impressed with Petran's efficiency, he did not like the man's manner. *I will just have to ask the Count about this room,* he thought.

"Yes, well, thank you for obtaining my supplies and fixing my meals for me, Petran."

"I do what the Master requires."

Again, the hostility was palpable under the surface. Wagner wondered at the odd choice of words. Petran's English was better than his—and with an educated enunciation. The man sounded as if he had attended university in England somewhere. Yet the word 'master' implied he was more a slave than a household servant or butler.

"Your English is quite good," Wagner observed.

Petran merely stared back at him.

"Right, well, thank you again." Wagner headed back for the spiral steps. When he had made it halfway up the long twisting staircase, he realized that Petran had not had a candle of his own. *I have left the fellow in the dark.* Petran was a surly one, no doubt, but Wagner was not keen on leaving the man blind in the cellar. Grudgingly, he turned and headed down the steps once more. He thought about how odd it was that he had not heard Petran come down the stairs. *But he must have seen my light.* Only two more rooms led off the stairs before he reached the cellar at the bottom, and those doors were open. He glanced inside each with his candle, looking for the tall servant, but both rooms were empty. As he reached the bottom step, he called out.

"Petran, my apologies, I did not mean to leave you in the dark."

But the wine cellar appeared empty.

Perplexed, Wagner spent a minute looking around the cellar for Petran, but not finding him, headed back to the stairs.

There must be another passage or room somewhere. Or maybe he is in the locked room with his secreted bottles. The last thought made Wagner smile. He made the long trudge up the steps to the kitchen, thinking about the strange servant.

Back in the foyer, he retrieved his wheelbarrow and rolled it out the front door to the courtyard. Earlier in the week he had tidied up the broad space, collecting salvageable bits of rubble and stone, and dumping the rest off the edge of the cliff, at the broken wall. The drop was vertiginous, and it presented quite a hazard, but he figured Petran and the Count had been living with the presence of that drop for some time, and it was nowhere near the front door to the castle. He had chosen to leave the opening in the wall to allow him to dispose of unwanted debris throughout the restoration. It would be one of the last things he fixed.

As he turned out the front door, the wheel on the cart making its routine squeak that had become so familiar to him that he had not bothered to oil it, he looked around the courtyard at the statues. He always looked at the statues. They were huge and dominated the courtyard, drawing the eyes up from the gray slabs of stone, made smooth with countless footfalls. The statues perplexed him, while at the same time filled him with dread. The two statues of ravens were overly large, as if some prehistoric bird had once inhabited the hills of Transylvania. The five statues of the old men with the flowing beards were stranger. They each wore different costumes or armor, indicating the men came from different periods of conflict throughout history. Each was armed with a spear or chipped sword. Wagner assumed they were the Count's ancestors. Each statue's eyes were the same though. Almost as if they were statues of the same man.

The Count himself only vaguely resembled these men. He had no beard, and his hair was shorter than the flowing locks on each statue's head. But when Wagner thought of the Count's eyes…yes, he could tell the Count was related to these ancient men. He thought the Count was an odd man, much older in his manner than his youthful appearance suggested. The man was introverted and dour at times, whereas at others he smiled wryly, seeing humor in things that Wagner did not. Still, the man was amiable enough, and he was paying Wagner very well. *I must keep my thoughts on the job.*

He pushed the wheelbarrow along the front wall of the building to the courtyard's edge, where the broken gray wall left a gap in the defenses to open blue sky, like a missing tooth in an otherwise flawless smile. At the edge, he paused and peered down the crag to the small hills far below. Low-lying clouds shrouded parts of the valley, but other patches of it were brilliant green and brown in the late morning sun. In two places, the beams of light were visible as slanted lines of light tearing down from the clouds and stabbing into the forests far below.

Beautiful, he thought. *Anneli will love it here. Well, maybe not the castle or that arrogant Petran, but the surrounding countryside…*

As he thought of his wife, he walked around the wheelbarrow to its handles and then rolled it forward toward the exposed edge of the courtyard. As he did, a chunk of rock the size of a human head fell off the pile of rubble and rolled back behind him, along the courtyard floor. He stopped the cart at the edge of the precipice and then turned and bent to reach for the fallen stone.

The action saved his life.

A huge piece of stone crashed down on the front edge of the wheelbarrow, popping the wooden handles up and banging Wagner on the chin, throwing him sprawling backward into the courtyard, before the cart, and all the stone it contained, flipped through the shattered wall and into the void. From his place on the stone floor of the courtyard, Wagner looked up to the top of the castle. At the top of the wall above him was one of the castle's many turrets. But he saw nothing to suggest how, or why, any stone might have fallen and nearly knocked him off the cliff.

I was just up there two days ago, and the stone was solid!

He strained his eyes to see movement, but detected nothing. *The stone must have just dislodged from somewhere I could not see from this vantage point, and fallen. Bad luck.* After his strange meeting with Petran, though, Wagner was inclined to suspect foul play. Large slabs of rock did not usually just fall. And he knew of very few incidents where they did so and nearly crushed or killed people. For some reason, when masonry failed, it always seemed to be in harsh storms or in the middle of the night—when most folks were sensibly indoors.

Wagner stood to his feet and walked across the courtyard to get a better view of the top of the castle's tower. He still saw nothing to suggest Petran's hand. He walked cautiously back to the gap in the courtyard wall, glancing upward frequently to check for danger, and peered over the edge. He could not even see the wheelbarrow at the bottom of the drop. He would have been killed, had he not reached for that loose stone.

He turned now and walked over to the stone that had nearly ended his life. He picked it up and took it with him as he headed for the tower to look for answers. Moments later, he emerged onto the roof of the tower, its low crenellated walls surrounding him. He stepped over to the edge that looked down to the roof of the castle and the courtyard in front of it. He could not see any place on the top of the tower from where the stone might have fallen. Nothing was loose around the retaining wall, and he even leaned over the sides of the walls in all four directions, and examined the walls below the tower. Then he looked at the huge chunk of stone in his hand.

Wherever you came from, it was not from up here. You're not even the same kind of stone.

CHAPTER ELEVEN

A week after the incident with the wheelbarrow, Wagner was walking on the road, having taken advantage of the beautiful day to stroll the few miles into the nearest village. As he walked, his mind drifted back to the incident. He had found nothing out of the ordinary in the tower, and his thoughts that Petran must have been behind the mysterious falling stones quickly faded. He hadn't seen Petran or the Count in many days, but he had left another list of supplies—including a request for a new wheelbarrow—and they had shown up the following day on or beside the breakfast table, with the new wheelbarrow waiting in the courtyard. He missed the old wheelbarrow's squeak, but the new one was sturdier. He also made sure to look up whenever he stepped out into the courtyard, but no other unusual items rained down from the heavens.

The previous day, he'd left a message on the kitchen table explaining his intention—weather permitting—to walk into the village today to examine the tools available at the small shop. He requested the coach be sent to bring him back to the castle at dusk. A terse note was waiting for him at breakfast reading only:

It will be done.
—P

So, with the usual hearty breakfast in his stomach, he had set off down the lone road toward the village. He figured it would take him a few hours to get there. The weather was lovely and the sun was just warm enough to make him comfortable. He smiled as he walked, and he welcomed the distance.

Out in the daylight, away from the gloomy castle, his thoughts turned to his wife and his original hopes that Hungary would provide a new start for them both. Maybe not in the castle or the xenophobic village, but in some small town along the river perhaps. Maybe in Dorna-Watra, the resort town. Many of the buildings and grounds there would need frequent upkeep to continually attract more tourists. And towns with money hired skilled craftsmen.

It felt good to be out walking again. He had spent many happy days in the hills and mountains of Europe. He hadn't realized how cooped up he felt in the castle until his boots were clopping along the rocky trail. The forest was dark with coniferous trees, some blue and some nearly black. Still, the shining sun lit the trail, and he whistled as he walked, feeling the oppressive weight of the castle lift from his shoulders with each step.

Soon enough, he was surprised when the road came out of the woods and into the empty fields. He was startled by their appearance and checked his watch to see whether he had been walking long. The village was small, and he assumed most of the folks farmed in the surrounding fields, although again, he noted that the fields further away from the town were untended. Only those tightly clustered around the village had been worked. He saw one or two men tending their small plots, or just walking in them, but these figures were too distant yet for Wagner to talk with them. When he remembered the hostile reception at the inn, he realized he really did not want to talk with these men anyway. He wanted to examine the tools in little town with the winding alleys. For all his love of books, Wagner was very much a man of his hands. He loved to work with tools, and he loved to examine them, assess them, and when he had the money to do so, buy them.

As he came along the dirt path into the center of the village, he noticed the ruined church again, and wondered why the villagers had never repaired it. The white steeple laid crumpled on the ground in front of the small building, and one side of the structure looked like it had simply fallen in. The remains of the white clapboard building had listed to the unaffected side. From the amount of debris, and the rot on the side of the wood cladding, Wagner guessed the building had been out of commission for years.

As he walked deeper into the little village, he spotted a few men folk and women, darting indoors at the sight of him. It was no more than he had expected. Still, he spied a small general store on his way into the village, and he suspected that was where Petran had been obtaining items for him. He determined to at least see what was on offer for sale in this remote locale.

The shop, at one end of town, was a small white building with a thatched roof, not entirely different from the inn or most of the other buildings. The sign, which had been hung above the door with perfect precision, was wood and proclaimed in German: *All Things*. Wagner noticed that this building was cleaner than the others, and he noted the cut grass and carefully tended flower bed in front of it. Whoever owned the store clearly took pride in maintaining its appearance.

He stepped through the door, and heard a small bell jingle on the inside of it. The inside of the shop was dim, but through no fault of the building's design—it was filled from floor to ceiling and from wall to wall with all manner of things in a seemingly haphazard fashion, and the huge stacks obscured the light from the windows. Books, sacks of flour and wheat, tools, clothes, fresh vegetables, cans of paint. It was all stacked in random and unpredictable ways, and the shop was larger on the inside than Wagner might have suspected from the outside. Narrow twisting paths led between the aisles of miscellaneous items, and the floor gave way to stairs down to a larger basement, which he imagined held even more.

No way can the interior of this shop be run by the same person that tends the outside, he thought.

The proprietor greeted him from behind the counter, and Wagner understood immediately. It was the Bavarian man with the pipe from the tavern. That explained the well-tended exterior of the building, but not the chaotic interior.

"Guten tag!" Wagner greeted the man in German.

"Ah! Herr Wagner, is it not? When we hadn't seen you in such a long time, we thought perhaps you had given up on your project at the castle." The man held his distinctive pipe in hand, but it was unlit. He had a thick beard that was going white, while his hair was still mostly dark with just streaks of light at the temples. His eyes were kind, with deep crinkles from a life of laughing. The brown suit he wore was slightly rumpled, with a colorful waistcoast under it. Wagner was reminded of university professors he had seen in Munich. "I am Henning Brandt," the man said. "Welcome to my shop."

Wagner took the offered hand. "You have quite an array of items for sale."

Brandt laughed. "Oh yes, I try to have a little of everything. We are far from the other towns and villages, so I try to bring in the odd thing from time to time. I actually have a system to how it's all arranged, I assure you. Just tell me what you need; I can find it for you."

"Just looking for shovels, hammers, any masonry tools you might have. Plus books, of course."

The older man's eyebrows raised. "You are a reader then, my friend? Come, I have much to show you."

Without waiting for a reply, Brandt turned and descended stairs at the back of the store to the broad basement, which to Wagner's estimation ran to a far wider footprint than that of the building. After some more shelving with various bric-a-brac, they entered a section of the shop that held only books. Aisles and aisles of shelves filled with bound volumes of every size. Wagner stopped in complete disbelief.

The Bavarian turned and looked at Wagner with sympathy. "I know. I bought many in my youth, and even though I know I'll never live long enough to read all of them, I keep buying more when I make trips to purchase supplies." He sighed, but there was good nature in it.

"So this is your personal collection, then?" Wagner asked.

"Yes, but I sell a few from time to time. Have a look around and let me know if you are looking for anything. The books are arranged in a logical fashion—even if everything upstairs is not." Herr Brandt laughed again and headed for the stairs as the bell on the front door jingled again.

Wagner began to examine the stacks and quickly decided it was a good thing the Count's library was so extensive, or he would be spending all of his pay here. Then he realized that the Count probably secured many of his recent volumes directly from Brandt. He decided to examine the books first and then ply the German for information about the village and the Count.

He was just pulling a book off the shelf to lose himself in another world—he had found a bound volume of old issues of Strand Magazine, and although the first issue in it contained the last Arthur Conan Doyle story *The Final Problem*, which he'd read, there were others in it he hadn't—when he recognized the clipped voice of the man addressing Brandt upstairs.

Petran.

CHAPTER TWELVE

Brandt didn't sound as if he liked Petran very much.

Where the old Bavarian had been kindly and gregarious with Wagner, he was brusque and all business with the tall, gangly servant. "No, I don't have any in stock. Anything else?"

"Yes, actually," Petran's carefully enunciated Oxford English sounded strange in the shop after Wagner had just been casually chatting with Brandt in German. "I would like to know if you have seen Herr Wagner today."

Wagner took an involuntary step back into the stacks of books in the basement at the mention of his name up in the shop.

"I have not." Brandt's answer surprised Wagner. "Are you expecting him? Should I give him a message if he comes in?"

A long silence followed. Then Petran spoke again, his tone somewhat petulant, "No message. Just these things, and any new books you have from the list."

The shrill ring of the hand-crank activating the cash register, and then Brandt gruffly replied, "No. Nothing new." A moment later a soft grunt and the door opened, chiming the shop's tiny bell. Wagner smiled to himself when the shopkeeper did not wish Petran a good day.

He stepped further back into the books and resumed his examination of the shelves, finding a few choice volumes that he pulled down to purchase. Twenty minutes later, the portly German came down the creaking steps to join him.

"You overheard?" The man spoke in their common Bavarian dialect.

"I did, Herr Brandt. It was Petran, was it not?" Wagner relished speaking to the man in their shared regional dialect. It meant that the man was opening up to him because of their familiar geographical history, but it also meant that their discussion would be almost unintelligible to any local Hungarians or Romanians that might overhear them. Although the standard German language was widely understood in this area, the Bavarian dialect would be challenging for anyone not a native speaker from that region.

"He is a slug. Always creeping, that one. He's one of my best customers, or I would turn him away entirely. He always asks for strange things I couldn't possibly have. Today it was live crickets." The man shrugged.

"Crickets?"

"Yes. He wanted a twenty-pound sack of them. Where am I supposed to get live crickets from? He sometimes buys loads of things at a go. Other times he is only looking for these kinds of odd things. But he pays in gold, so I tolerate him."

Wagner absorbed the comment about Petran paying in gold. The Count was clearly doing well in his consulting business, so the gold made sense. Only the wealthy would be likely to call on him to consult on obscure diseases.

Brandt stepped closer, and his expression went from amusedly exasperated to deadly serious, "He was asking after you."

"The Count's coach is supposed to collect me this afternoon," Wagner told him. "I suppose he was hoping to save a journey in from the castle, but I've only just got here, and now that I see your selection of books…" Wagner held up the armload he had already collected for purchase.

Brandt smiled a small bibliophile's smile and took out his pipe. He began to load the bowl with a fragrant tobacco.

"Have you met him yet?" he asked. The smile evaporated.

"The Count? Yes. A few times. Much younger than I would have suspected." Wagner watched as the shopkeeper lit the pipe and took a few tentative puffs of smoke. Normally, Wagner would have wanted to avoid pipe smoke in such a confined space, but he actually found the tobacco quite pleasant.

"Younger?" Brandt raised an eyebrow. "When we last saw him here in the village, he was an old man."

"Perhaps, this man is the former's son, then?" Wagner offered.

"Perhaps. Let's hope so. The father was a nasty man."

Wagner waited, hoping there would be some elaboration, but the older Bavarian turned and headed for the stairs. After another thirty minutes perusing the shelves—and finding several more volumes to purchase, some new and others with cracked leather bindings—Wagner returned to the shop's upper level. He looked through the miscellaneous items on the shelves for a few minutes. He quickly gave up on deciphering any semblance of logic in the organization. He asked Brandt for assistance, and then explained to the man the kind of restoration work he was doing on the old castle. Although the man had no stone-working experience, he quickly grasped the scope of the work and began suggesting tools and items that were mostly of use. Wagner would be leaving with far more items than he had intended to. The discussion quickly ranged back to Bavaria, and things both men had seen and done in Munich. When Wagner revealed his penchant for climbing in the Alps, he discovered Brandt had been a climber as well.

"It's why I came to this country in the first place. In retrospect, I should have gone to Switzerland." Brandt went on to tell the tale of how he had come to Transylvania, and regaled Wagner with his climbing exploits. Before either man knew it, they had been talking for hours, and along the way they had become friends.

Wagner checked his battered watch and announced that he needed to go because the Count's coach would be coming for him. He noted that Brandt frowned at the mention of the coach. He wondered if it was because they had enjoyed such a great discussion, which had now come to an end, or if it was because he had mentioned the owner of the coach. Whatever it was that had happened between the Count's father—*it had to have been his father,* Wagner thought, *the man is barely thirty*—and the people of the village, Wagner determined to learn of it, but he knew it would take time. Brandt seemed to be his best bet. Certainly the other villagers he had met were too hostile to ever open up.

He arranged with Brandt to have his items collected by Petran, who, it turned out, visited the village every other day to collect food and supplies. Brandt had also mentioned that Petran was his largest purchaser of books, often leaving long lists of titles for the Bavarian to collect on his travels. Brandt didn't like Petran, and he rarely spoke of the Count, but he did admire their taste in books. He admitted that he hadn't been sure of the Count's return and sometimes wondered if Petran was the heavy reader. Brandt said the money he had earned just from selling books to the Count could have allowed him to start another shop. Instead he used the money to travel to the great cities of Europe once a year, seeking out rare new volumes for himself and for the Petran's list.

"Have a very wonderful day, Herr Brandt. I look forward to our next discussion. I shall try to come in to the village far more often now." Wagner smiled warmly, and the older Bavarian smiled back at him as he stepped out of the store and into the village sunlight.

The sun was low in the sky, but it was still a bright day. Wagner wrestled with the stack of books he had purchased that he felt he couldn't do without until Petran's next journey into the village. He began walking toward the inn, suddenly famished. The food had been good that first night; he could tolerate the surly proprietor's disgruntled attitude if it meant another fine meal.

He had taken only a few steps when he spied Petran a few buildings down, stepping out of a door that had a sign swinging over it in the shape of a loaf of bread. Petran's dark suit and gangly frame stood in contrast to the white-washed buildings and the glare of the sun. His hair was greasy, and it shone in the glinting beams of sunshine slicing through the clouds above. He looked altogether awkward and uncomfortable out in the daylight, nothing like the confrontational man Wagner had met in the wine cellar at the castle. Petran hadn't noticed him, and turned to walk toward the narrow black coach parked further up the lane. Wagner considered following Petran to explain his desire to eat before returning to the castle, but changed his mind. *No, he can just wait for me.*

He was about to turn back for the door to Miklos's tavern when a strong hand gripped his shoulder from behind and an arm wrapped around his throat.

CHAPTER THIRTEEN

Andreas Wagner twisted, his attacker's grip loosening, and he swung his pile of books, bringing them up to smash his attacker's face. The man released him and stepped back, the blow with the stack of books missing him. Wagner tightened his grip on the layers of books in his arms. His surprise and anger at the assault quickly turned to elation when he took in the sight of his attacker.

"Fritz!" he shouted. "Damn, man, you scared the life out of me."

Fridtjof Bischoff was a large man with good Germanic looks. Blonde hair cut short like a soldier's and blue eyes as clear as blue-tinged glass. He stood almost a head taller than Wagner, and was easily twice as broad. Where Wagner was lank and corded muscle, Fritz was beefy bulk, liberally covered with a thin layer of fat from extensive and happy beer drinking. As usual, he wore a waistcoat with no jacket. Wagner could not recall Fritz ever wearing a jacket.

"What are you doing here?" Wagner smiled at his old friend as he adjusted his stack of books to one arm, and vigorously shook Fritz's offered hand.

"We decided to come over a bit early and surprise you. The job is still on, right?" Fritz unloaded some of Wagner's stack of books, and tucked them in his armpit.

"Of course it is. Wait... 'we'?" Wagner quickly turned around to see his wife emerging from the door of Miklos's inn.

Anneli Wagner was a vision of beauty. Her brilliant yellow dress made her stand out against the white of the village buildings and the green of the fields down the road beyond them. Her long blonde hair was pulled back in a neat bow, and her eyes glittered like cut gemstones. Her smile washed over her face as she saw Wagner, and she began to rush across the road to him.

They embraced, and he held his mute wife with a sudden and desperate longing. He hadn't realized how much he had missed her, but now that she was in his arms, he felt the emotion spread over him. From the tightness of her embrace, he could tell the experience was the same for her. When she at last pulled away from his hug, and Wagner became aware of Fritz's good-natured laughter behind him, he could see Anneli's eyes were wet with tears, and her silent mouth was turned up in a joyous smile.

"I've missed you deeply, my love," he told her softly.

She nodded.

"I wish Fritz would talk like that to me some day!" the new voice was high and a little grating, but Wagner was glad to hear it. He stepped back from Anneli's embrace to see Gretchen standing next to Fritz. She had a long rope of dark hair that stretched down to her waist, and soft brown eyes. She wore a dress similar to Anneli's, but hers was a faint blue, and Wagner wasn't sure the color fit her. She would frequently wear daring dresses with very low-cut fronts, but this one was less revealing. Wagner thought her pretty, but in a plain sort of way. She was very slim and had narrow hips and a slightly pointed nose. She was a lively and fun girl, who had made Fritz happy for the last year, and who had been a constant companion for Anneli after the loss of Britta. Wagner would have been forever grateful to the woman for that alone, but through her association with Fritz, she had become his friend as well.

"And there you are, you gorgeous thing! Is this lunkish brute treating you right?" Wagner instantly fell into the harmless flirting he and Gretchen had always engaged in.

"She's keeping me constantly busy with her shopping sprees across the fine stores of Europe, if you must know," Fritz complained. Wagner knew that the woman liked to shop. She sheepishly copped to it, with a smile, and Wagner laughed.

"I wasn't expecting the three of you for another few weeks. Why the change?"

"We got bored after Gretchen had us all packed and ready to go two weeks ago," Fritz joked.

Gretchen playfully slapped at the big man's arm.

"Well," Wagner thought for a moment, "I haven't arranged transportation for everyone, and the road is quite narrow." He spied the coach from Dorna-Watra parked at the north end of town, and the Count's narrow coach waiting for him at the south end of town. There was no sign of Petran now. "There's no way your coach can make the journey."

Fritz stepped up closer as he looked at the narrow coach Wagner pointed to. "Well, then, we'll just have to send the ladies on in that narrow little thing, and you and I will ride the horses from the bigger coach."

Wagner was about to ask whether such a thing would be acceptable for the coachman that had brought them to the village, but Fritz was already sauntering over to the man. Wagner smiled. His friend was wealthy, of course, and didn't really need the Count's employment. Fritz would just bribe the coach driver, and if that failed, he would buy the horses outright.

Fritz had agreed to come to Transylvania with the ladies, to make Wagner's acceptance of the position with the Count a little easier. He had offered to help Wagner find local work, but after the death of his daughter, Wagner had initially lost any drive to perform work, but then when it returned, he was determined to start anew in a different locale. Besides, Wagner could never accept charity from his friend, and he knew that Fritz understood that, too, but the man had been decent enough to make the offer, regardless.

Wagner stood with the ladies for a few minutes while Fritz worked his magic with the coachman. Gretchen chatted nearly non-stop, and Wagner made the appropriate noises in reply, but his eyes kept darting to his wife, and she kept returning his looks with a sly smile. She seemed healthier already, in the few weeks they had been apart. Maybe the change of scenery was doing her good. *Maybe she will even speak again soon*, he thought.

"I suggest we step into the inn and order some food before the journey. It's not far, but I am famished."

"An excellent idea!" Gretchen said, and led them toward to door to the inn. Anneli lingered behind her for just a moment, smiling at Wagner, and he leaned in to place a gentle kiss on her cheek. Then she took his arm and they followed Gretchen into the small tavern.

Surly Miklos was at his post at the worn front desk, but a different girl was waiting the tables. Even though it was early afternoon, many of the same village men were already seated in the tavern and looking, with their steins of beer, as if they were settled in for the night.

"Hello, Herr Miklos. Can we get food for four? Your cooking the last time I was here, a few weeks ago, was so excellent, I thought I should introduce my friends to it."

The man recognized Wagner and began to nod. Then he saw Anneli and Gretchen, and he looked stricken.

He pointed to Anneli. "Is...is this your wife, Herr Wagner?"

"Yes," Wagner was suddenly suspicious of Miklos's unusual interest. "My wife, Anneli Wagner. Dear, this is Herr Miklos, who runs this establishment. Is something wrong, Herr Miklos?"

The man composed himself and quickly replied, "No, sir. No. Nothing wrong. It's just that it can be quite dangerous in the mountains for a woman, as I told you the last time we met."

"I understand. In fact, I myself, had a brush with danger up at the castle, when a loose piece of masonry nearly crushed me." Anneli whipped her head around to look at him with concern in her eyes. He gently laid his hand on her arm to assuage her. "I was fine, however." He turned his eyes back to the innkeeper. "I've been making many improvements on the place, and while the journey up there is indeed perilous, I suspect we will all be fine."

"Of course we'll be fine!" Fritz's voice boomed as he entered the tavern. "Drinks for everyone, barkeep! On me!"

This was met with a round of applause. *He knows how to win a hostile room*, Wagner thought. Indeed, the usually grouchy, fear-stricken men in the room were quite happy now.

CHAPTER FOURTEEN

They ate quickly, knowing dusk was coming. The treacherous road to the castle would become even more deadly in the dark.

As they left the tavern, many of the patrons thanked Fritz, but some were so far into their drink, they could only nod or drool on the tables where they slept. Outside, the sun was already set behind the mountains, but light still filled the sky. The wide coach's driver had been inside with them, drinking with the others. He joined them outside and released two of his four horses from their traces for Wagner and Fritz to ride. He explained that he had already transferred the luggage to Petran's narrow coach, and indeed, the black narrow carriage was parked close to the inn's door. Petran, gloomy, stood scowling in the deepening dusk. As soon as he saw the group approaching, he spoke.

"We must hurry. The light fails." He turned and climbed up to the driver's seat. Fritz helped the ladies into the black carriage, while Wagner took possession of the chestnut brown horses from the other coach driver. He climbed atop his steed, and held the reins of the second horse for Fritz. His job done, the coachman headed back into the inn, where Wagner supposed he would spend the night happily drinking Fritz's money away.

Fritz stepped away from the narrow black coach to address Wagner. "Are you ready, my friend?"

Just then Petran snapped the reins, and the two obsidian stallions that sat at the front of the black carriage raced off down the road at top speed, just as they had done when Wagner had taken his original journey to the castle. Fritz was startled by the narrow coach's sudden departure.

"He's an impatient fellow, isn't he?"

"Come on, Fritz. We've no time to lose if we are to catch up to them." Wagner nudged his horse to step toward Fritz, and the other came horse with him.

Fritz took the reins to his own horse and swept up onto the back of his steed, as if he were born to do so. Wagner was no stranger to riding, but he admired the smooth grace of his friend's way with animals. Fritz and beasts always took a liking to one another.

Pulling his coat closed against the chill air, Wagner put his heels into the mare. He and the horse took off down the dirt road in the oncoming dimness, and Fritz followed. They chased the coach through the alpine pastures, with it always just at the edge of sight. Wagner was surprised that no matter how fast he urged his horse onward, they were not able to catch up with the speeding black carriage in the distance.

When the fields gave way to gray rocky passages through the stone of the mountain, the deepening dusk already resembling the night and lit only by the brilliant starshine above them in the clear sky, Fritz pulled up by Wagner's side.

"The man is flying! How will we catch him?"

It was then that Wagner recalled his first trip along the road and his walk on it earlier in the day.

"Fritz! Ride behind me, the road narrows to just a strip!" Wagner called.

Fritz glanced ahead and saw the danger just in time. He pulled back hard on his reins and his mare skittered and sputtered to a stop on the loose stone, as Wagner shot forward along the twisting path, as the wall of stone on their left disappeared to leave nothing but open sky on that side of them. Wagner wanted to glance again to the castle, but he didn't dare take his eyes from the road, which was becoming difficult to see in the gloom.

Shortly, he could hear Fritz's snorting steed just behind him on the trail. When they entered the thick forest, the night closed in around them like a cloak, and Wagner had to trust that his horse could find the way. He could see only the occasional glint of starshine off the branches of trees that reached out into the path. By the time he saw them, they were already whipping at his body as he blasted past them. His thoughts of being cold were gone now. The excitement of the chase and the hard riding was causing him to sweat.

They burst out of the forest and onto the long, twisting stripe of raised rock that acted as a natural bridge to the castle in the distance. The moon was full, but sat low over the horizon beyond the castle and the hills. It lit their way like a giant version of Wagner's electric flashlight. Wagner could see the carriage just reaching the castle's gates ahead. With more light to see, he urged his horse on faster along the tiny road, with Fritz still close on his heels.

As the two men raced through the castle's gates into the darkened courtyard, Wagner could just see Anneli emerging from the coach's door. Her face looked pale in the beam of the white moonlight. Petran was already out of sight. Pulling hard on the reins, Wagner pulled his mare up just shy of the carriage, its hooves scraping on the worn smooth stone floor of the wide courtyard.

Gretchen was stepping out of the coach now, letting a very unladylike stream of choice words for her driver flow from her mouth, as if she were a Hamburg dock worker. Wagner had to smile. Fritz pulled up, dismounting, patting the horse long and hard as the beast breathed in terrible gulps after the fast run.

"Anneli, are you alright?" Wagner asked, moving to his wife. She was walking around the courtyard's shadows as if in a daze. She took a step toward him, and something swooped at him out of the darkness.

It knocked him backward against the carriage. He struck at it with an arm, and the creature darted back.

The foul creature screeched with a shrill, ear-piercing wail,
and swooped in for another attempt at his throat.

It was a bat. A huge bat with a wingspan of at least a yard. Wagner's hand darted to his neck, where the thing had scratched at him with its claws.

The foul creature screeched with a shrill, ear-piercing wail, and swooped in for another attempt at his throat. Its small eyes reflected the moonlight in a fiery shade of red. Fritz stepped up and clubbed the flying animal with his arm. It fluttered away to the far side of the courtyard and up into the sky, screeching all the while.

"Mein Gott! Did you see the size of that thing?" Fritz said.

"It nearly took my head off," Wagner said, running to Anneli, who only now looked as if she were snapping out of the daze she had been in. "Are you alright, my dear?"

She blinked a few times, as if working away sleepiness, then turned to him and smiled a soft reassuring smile. Yes, she would be fine, it said.

Darkness had fallen completely on the courtyard now, with the moon slipping behind a cloud. Fritz looked amused at the escapade. Gretchen looked terrified. Anneli looked simply tired. Wagner rubbed his hand at his throat, feeling the scratches that hadn't drawn blood, but which would leave a mark.

"Let us get indoors, my friends."

CHAPTER FIFTEEN

The men settled the ladies with their own rooms. Despite Wagner and Anneli being married, Fritz and Gretchen were not. The decision was made to avoid any signs of impropriety, despite the fact that Wagner had lied to the Count and referred to Gretchen as Fritz's wife. With the castle having as many unused rooms as it did, the choice seemed optimal to all four of them.

With both women safely ensconced in Gretchen's room, Fritz and Wagner left to make arrangements with Petran for food for all of them in the morning—or as Wagner explained to Fritz, to leave a written request for the normally invisible servant. As the door to the room closed, Gretchen turned to Anneli like an excited school girl. "Did you see the size of that bat? My goodness! It was so horrible!"

Anneli nodded dutifully. Although conversation was beyond her means, she would nod and smile, and Gretchen would hold up both sides of the conversation on her own just fine.

"This place is amazing, though. I wonder what the mysterious Count looks like. Did Andreas describe him?" Gretchen prattled as she began unpacking clothes from her valise.

Anneli shrugged from her seat on the bed. Gretchen didn't even see the movement, but continued on as if she had.

"I bet he's old and crusty. Or maybe he's a delicious young man with dark eyes and moody, pouty lips."

Anneli looked sharply at her friend, but Gretchen was still going on about her fantasies while putting away her belongings. Anneli had dreamt of the Count in Munich—a young man with dark eyes and sensual lips. Nearly exactly the way Gretchen had described the man. She wondered for a moment whether it was possible they had both shared some kind of dream, but then she dismissed the notion. She smiled to herself. The image of their mysteriously absent host was simply a schoolgirl stereotype—the tall, dark, European image of royalty. A prince to sweep a woman off her feet and onto his beautiful horse. She laughed to herself at the ludicrousness of it. And what would she need of a man like that?

Her thoughts turned to her husband. Thoughtful, hard working, pleasant, and gentle. He was clever and shrewd with money. He was also a very handsome man. He wasn't royalty, or wealthy, by any stretch of her imagination, but Andreas had provided for her and their child. Her thoughts darkened momentarily at the thought of her lost baby, her *Britta*, but she quickly turned those thoughts away to more pleasant things, as she had learned to do. She could dwell on the horrors of what had happened to her baby or she could move on. It had been a year. It was time for her to start thinking forward. She and Andreas would have other children. They had traveled across the mountains of Europe to come to this new land of farms and craggy rocks to begin again. She knew her husband's heart was in the right place. His solution was to break from nearly everything and start again anew. Somewhere else. Something different. She was grateful that approach had not applied to her. *He could very well have left me, too.* But that was not the sort of man he was. Besides, she could tell that he was still madly in love with her, and she still loved him deeply as well. No, she didn't need any mystery men. Her husband was her world, and together they would find their way into the future.

"…he's just afraid to commit and seal the deal. But I told him, 'Fritzie, this thing is good for you and for me.

We should just go with them to Transylvania for the fun of it.' I told him the change of climate would be good for both of us, and once separated from his familiar environs in Munich, he would see how much he needed me. I'm sure marriage will follow soon."

Gretchen had managed to put away most of her belongings, even positioning her hairbrush and hand mirror on the dressing table just so, before she turned to Anneli for approval.

"He will ask me soon, don't you think?" Gretchen's face began to fall, as if without Anneli's agreement, her entire constructed fantasy would crumble. Anneli knew this approach from her friend quite well. She smiled widely, and nodded enthusiastically for her friend, while privately thinking to herself, *Not a chance, Gretch. He'll probably have moved on to a new woman—or twenty—before the year is up.* She liked Fritz, but she knew his type, and she knew that Gretchen wasn't it. She had probably seemed it on the surface. Pretty, curvy, and readily willing. But if Gretchen's nonstop babbling annoyed her, what must it be doing to Fritz? She had spied him a few times with that helpless look on his face she had seen cuckolded men in Munich wear. He hid the look well, when he knew she or Andreas were looking at him. Especially when he knew that Gretchen was looking at him. But she had seen it often enough to know it for what it was. That look, combined with his appreciative appraisals of other women on the sly? He would soon be looking for a way out. She knew his pattern.

Anneli put her hand on her friend's arm and patted gently. Gretchen was mollified and smiled widely, before embarking on her next topic of discussion. Anneli shook her head to herself. She would listen for another half an hour or so before demurring and indicating with a yawn that she needed to go to her bedroom.

Then she would instead go to her husband's room. *Propriety be damned.*

Gretchen was arranging some of her extensive jewelry collection on her dressing table, and going on about the home she and Fritz would have in the Bavarian country after the job here in Transylvania was done.

Maybe I need to make that yawn sooner rather than later, Anneli thought.

She stepped over to her friend, and a gleam of candlelight reflected off a tiny glittering chain and a plain silver cross on the end of it. The desk was covered with more and nicer pieces of jewelry, but the reflection of light hit her eye, and Anneli reached out to pick up the cross. Gretchen noticed, and stopped her incessant talking to sadly examine her friend. Anneli rubbed the silver of the cross with her thumb, before noticing Gretchen's attention.

"You like that one, Sweetie? I haven't worn it for ages. Here, let's put it on you." Gretchen took the cross and slid the delicate chain around Anneli's neck and clasped it with the practiced hands of an expert jeweler.

Anneli looked at herself in the mirror. The tip of the cross rested just at the bottom edge of her ample cleavage, the light glittering off the necklace and drawing the eye irresistibly to her feminine charms. She smiled, with thoughts of her reunion with her husband going through her head. Gretchen misunderstood her entirely.

"You look wonderful, dear. You keep that one. It suits you far better than it ever suited me. Oh, Anneli, I just know things are going to get better for you."

CHAPTER SIXTEEN

Gretchen startled when the door behind her opened. Anneli had left her almost an hour ago. She had just been changing into her nightgown, and quickly pulled her dress up off the table and held it in front of her as a shield.

The door swung wide open, and a man with dark hair stepped into the room. Gretchen had no idea who this man was, and she was about to scream. She could feel the scream crawling up her throat, about to pounce onto her tongue for its lunge past her teeth. But the scream stopped at the back of her throat, when the man lifted his face to her, and their eyes locked. The eyes were dark, but she could not look away, as if they were sucking her in, pulling her toward them.

The man stepped into the room, and the door closed behind him. He swept toward her, then stopped, tilting his head slightly. His eyes held her like a magnet reaching out for the iron in her soul. He was gorgeous. Young, and handsome, wearing an open dark suit, with a white waistcoat, and a high-collared shirt. His long black hair framed his white skin, and his mouth was a tight line on his face, the lips bloodless. His look portrayed need and lust, and she instantly found herself wanting him.

She dropped the dress she was holding in front of her nightgown, now showing this strange man her form through just the one layer of cloth. She found it hard to breathe, and wanted so much to know the man, to fall forever into his embrace.

"Come," he said. His voice was powerful, and brooked no argument, yet the tone was no more than a hissing whisper.

Gretchen walked slowly toward him, as if in a daze. She wasn't controlling her own feet, even though they took her precisely where she wanted to go—into the arms of this handsome, mysterious man, with all thoughts of Fritz having vanished from her mind. She wanted to ask his name. To ask him a million questions, but each one fell away from her thoughts as it occurred to her. Although normally one of the most talkative women she knew, she found herself without anything meaningful to say. The only thing that mattered was his stare. His touch.

Him.

The man reached one arm around her waist slowly, gliding the hand along her back like the dusk settling over the land of her spine. When his hand reached fully around behind her and to her side, he tugged on her, launching her body up against the front of his. She gasped at the surprise. She could feel his manhood, stiff and pulsing and he pressed up against her stomach. She was looking up at the smooth skin of his chin—not a single hair on his white face. His eyes were looking down at her, and when her eyes climbed up his face to his lower eyelashes, she was trapped once again in those swirling pools of ebony. But somewhere deep in the murky depths of those holes into night, she saw a twinkling illumination. A kindling fire that spread up the sides of the blackness, reaching out for her.

Now she grew frightened, and she wanted to look away, but his other hand was roaming around her body, while he still forcefully held her body close to him. His eyes still kept hers prisoner. She watched the fires in his mind grow. She understood that this man was going to indulge her every fantasy and leave her exhausted. She wanted that fiercely, but she was frightened as well. Her voice made a small squeaking noise, and his lips were on hers, his tongue probing her mouth with urgent need.

She kissed him back, now with a growing need of her own. His arm holding her released from around her waist, freeing the hand to caress her breasts. When his hand found the neckline of her nightgown, he began to tug on it. To her surprise, her own hand was on the other side, helping him to tear the fabric from her body. The gown came away in a loud shredding rip, but she kissed him harder, and threw her arms around his neck, as the tattered garment fell away to the floor.

Suddenly his arms were under her, and she was being carried to the bed. She pulled at his shirt and waistcoat. Then she was on the bed, his eyes capturing her completely, yet again. The coal black was gone. It had ignited into a fiery swirling red or blood and flame. She found herself reaching forward with her head, and her lips kissed his eye, the eyelid fluttering closed a second before the skin of her lower lip touched the shining orb.

His clothes were gone, and the candles in the room were all nearly extinguished. One lone flame spit and hissed in the corner of the room, on a tiny wooden three-legged table. She reached for his lower back and pulled him toward her. Shadows danced around the bed like living things, wrapping themselves around this man like streaming silk lovers.

She had a tiny flickering thought that what she was doing was wrong. It slipped into her consciousness and slid around her mind, like a slippery bar of soap. Then she caught it. She had it. She needed her voice. To use her voice. She needed it. She focused on the idea and pushed. And then it was there in her mouth.

Not a scream or the protest she had expected. Her mouth betrayed her. Her lips broke away from his, and she drew in a deep breath.

"Yes," she said.

Then he was in her, and she was floating in a cloud-filled paradise of pleasure and yearning. She wrapped her legs and arms around him tightly, pulling him in and breathing in rhythm with him. The shadows began to envelop her as they did him. The light in the room was fading. She was soaring, and every part of her was screaming in delight and ecstasy.

She felt him lunge deeper into her, and the candle in the corner finally gave up its last dying light. The blackness took them, and she whispered again and again.

"Yes."

The pleasure was all. The room, the blackness, the scent of the burnt-out candle, the tickle of his coarse hair as it draped along her face, and eventually even the pain.

It was all a part of the pleasure.

CHAPTER SEVENTEEN

The following day the men went out to work directly after breakfast. Wagner had mentioned the Count's extensive library while they ate and Gretchen, distracted through most of the meal, vowed that the women would explore it immediately. Almost as if she had been waiting for a moment to get Anneli alone.

Wagner gave Fritz a brief tour of the castle to examine areas he thought they might work on in the coming weeks. Fritz offered a few ideas, but mostly nodded and agreed with Wagner. When they had completed the tour, he suggested they start with the courtyard where Wagner had nearly been crushed.

"Actually, I thought we'd use that opening in the wall to dump debris. Let's save it for later. But you are right—with the winter coming on, we should get the outdoor work done first."

They settled on shoring up the small stone walls that lined the entrance to the natural bridge to the castle from the nearby cliffs. They would be outdoors in the good weather and would get to examine the castle from across the chasm, looking for any additional exterior areas Wagner had not yet noted.

The gloomy day passed uneventfully, as the men worked with pick and shovel, and then with stone and trowel. The sky continually threatened rain, but none came from the leaden clouds. They came back to the castle for lunch with the women. Gretchen, wearing an emerald green gown with lace and frills, dominated the conversation with gushing adoration for the Count's library. Anneli, now wearing a bright sky-blue dress with a modest neckline, nodded and smiled at all the right times, but Wagner could tell she was bored with the books and with Gretchen. More than once he saw her look at him with a tiny gleam in her eye. He could tell she was recalling their passionate reunion lovemaking the previous night. Toward the end of the lunch, Wagner determined to call a halt to the day's efforts with Fritz earlier than normal, so that he might find his way to his lovely wife's bed with energy remaining for the night ahead.

Fritz had been a lively conversationalist throughout the morning, but after they returned across the natural stone pathway to the other side of the cavern to appraise the castle and resume work on the wall, the large man fell silent. Wagner wondered if his friend was just feeling the post-meal bloat and needed a nap, or whether something was bothering him. They had been friends for years and could joke with each other about most aspects of their lives, but when it came to serious talk about what was bothering them, both men would usually clam up. Instead of simply asking, Wagner analyzed what he had seen from his friend in the last day.

Fritz had been merry and his typical outgoing self, even taking the incident with the bat in stride. But he had said little to Gretchen, Wagner realized. Then again, Gretchen usually did most of the talking. The two made a pretty good couple, Wagner thought, because they both enjoyed the same kind of carefree life, eating out at fine restaurants in the city one week, then launching off on a months-long journey to the far reaches of Hungary the next to help a friend with a construction project. After they were done here, they had talked of making a visit to America.

Gretchen was fun, even if she talked a bit too much, and she was quite pretty. She and Fritz had been an item for most of a year now. With her being Anneli's friend, and Fritz being his, those two had naturally gravitated toward each other. She appeared happy enough to be here...so *what is the problem*, Wagner wondered.

And then he knew.

"She wants to get married, doesn't she?" he asked his friend.

Fritz didn't turn to Wagner, but continued to walk further along the narrow raised strip of land that formed a winding bridge to the castle. "She says we've been together long enough. She thinks that our time here will make me see that I don't need the nightlife of Munich. She wants us to marry and move to the countryside. Maybe somewhere in the Black Forest." Fritz kicked at a loose stone on the walkway, and it sailed out into the void. The drop down to the valley floor was hundreds of yards, possibly a mile down. The edge of the ribbon of land was steep, but a few scraggly trees grew from the sides of it, before the land sloped outward to a more gradual hill. It then dropped away, hundreds of feet lower to the river far below the castle. Fritz stood staring at his kicked rock, watching it for what felt to Wagner like forever.

Wagner understood his friend and needed no further information. Fritz was a social creature. The notion of being locked away on a small farm with only Gretchen for conversation would destroy him. Fritz was always the popular man in the tavern—not only because he freely bought drink for strangers, but because he loved to meet new people and hear their stories. He told some of the tallest tales, and was always the life of a party. Although Wagner could see himself settling down with Anneli in some remote part of Germany someday, he knew that to remove Fritz from the life of the city for too long would remove the essence of who Fritz was. After a few months here at the castle working on rock, the man would be ready to flee back to Vienna or Budapest. Wagner had always known that Fritz's help, while valuable and fun, would probably not last for the duration of the restoration project. He had planned for that, and he knew to get any work that required two sets of hands done quickly, so Fritz could be free to depart when he felt ready.

Wagner frowned at the thought that Gretchen could have been with Fritz for a year and not known the man well enough to see he could never be happy with that kind of life. *Maybe she's so busy talking all the time, she never takes the time to hear what Fritz has to say. Or maybe he just doesn't say it.* The latter was more likely, the more Wagner thought about it.

"You'll have to tell her. You'll have to—" Wagner began.

But Fritz cried out. A startled shout.

Wagner spun around to look for his friend on the bridge, but the man was gone. He raced several yards to where Fritz had been standing. When he looked over the edge of the wall, he saw his friend. Twenty feet down the wall, Fritz hung from one arm on a jagged brown tree branch that jutted out from the soil on the side of the wall.

"I need to run to the castle to get rope, Fritz. Try to hold on."

"Go, I'll be fine. But Andreas?"

Wagner had started to go, but stopped and looked over the edge of the precipitous fall again. "Yes?"

"Hurry." Fritz smiled, but the smile was grim and suggested he was in pain.

Wagner sprinted down the twisting ribbon of rock and soil toward the castle. He had a large coil of rope in his new wheelbarrow, just inside the outer courtyard. He made a wide turn inside and snatched it up on his way back out again, not having slowed his run at all. When he reached the edge of the wall where Fritz had fallen, he could see that Fritz had raised and hooked a leg over the jutting twisted tree, to ease the strain on his shoulder, but the man still looked intensely uncomfortable.

Wagner quickly wrapped the rope around himself and made a rescue loop on the other end, with a one-handed bowline. He lowered the makeshift lasso to his friend and then kept his eyes on the man until he saw the rope secured. Fritz outweighed him, so he sat back away from the edge, with one foot braced on a natural boulder embedded in the ground atop the road, which had been incorporated into the man-made wall, probably because removing it would have been too much work. Fritz would have to climb—there was no way Wagner could pull him up. Both men knew that, and no communication would be necessary. But Wagner had examined the wall and soil along the twenty-foot drop to the gnarled tree. Fritz would have no easy time of it, so Wagner would need to keep him on tight tension for most of the climb, and he might even need to take all of Fritz's 200 pounds of weight if the man fell.

He braced himself against the boulder, and pulled in slack on the rope whenever he felt it. The rope tugged a few times and Wagner knew Fritz was in danger, but he struggled against the pull and held fast to the line. After a moment, the rope would slacken again. Fritz would know he couldn't leave his weight on the rope for long. Covered in sweat now, Wagner leaned back away from the boulder on which he had placed both feet. He was nearly lying down on the road of the natural bridge, his eyes staring at the heavy clouds in the sky, as he strained.

Finally, he heard a grunt at the edge of the road and glanced down by his legs to see Fritz's arm outstretched and scrabbling for purchase.

"To your right. A crack." Wagner offered.

Fritz's hand slid to the side like a crab, and his fingers slid into a rock opening in the floor of the road. Next came Fritz's leg, and then he pulled himself up onto the road. Wagner felt the rope go completely slack. Only then did he move from his stance and roll over to grab his friend by the arm. Fritz winced briefly, and Wagner knew the shoulder had been damaged in the fall. He released his grasp and rolled over onto his back, breathing equally as heavily as Fritz.

"You need to watch your step around here."

"Nothing wrong with my step. I was pushed." Fritz said through heavy gasps.

Wagner sat up and looked at his friend.

"Not you," Fritz assured. "You were far too far away. But trust me, I felt something shove me hard in the back before I went over."

Both men looked along the winding road toward the castle.

"But there was no one else here on the road with us," Wagner said.

"That might be, but I'll be able to show you the bruise from where I got hit. Maybe another angry beast?"

Wagner thought about it, then looked over the other side of the bridge, away from where Fritz had fallen. He wondered if there might be a secret passage under the road. Another massive bat was a long shot. His money was on the arrogant Petran.

CHAPTER EIGHTEEN

Back in his unfamiliar room in the castle that evening, Fritz set his broken fob watch down on a writing desk, and removed his waistcoat. He replayed the events of the day that had led to his sore shoulder. *Sore? Wrenched out of the socket is more like it*, he thought. He mentally ran through the situation again and again. Andreas had been much too far away along the stone road—almost at the cliff. There had been no secret stairs. The men had checked. No nearby trees, where a falling branch might have hit Fritz in the lower spine, sending him reeling off the side of the road. It hadn't even been particularly windy.

Nonetheless, Fritz was certain someone or something had pushed him. He had felt the shove in his lower back before he had sailed out over the void. Only the sheer luck of the placement of the tree and his quick grasp of its limb had saved his life. That, and his friend's reaction time. Andreas had mentioned the strange behavior of the coach driver, Petran, but Fritz could not believe a man could move so quickly—and in so exposed an area—as to not be seen at all.

His own theory was that the giant bat from the night before had returned.

In any case, he was lucky to be alive, as Gretchen had told them all repeatedly at dinner that night. He had excused himself immediately after eating so he could retire to his bed. He wanted to rest his shoulder, but he also wanted no more of Gretchen's endless yammering.

He reclined on the bed, having managed only to take off his shirt before giving up on removing the trousers. The shoulder was throbbing and he needed to close his eyes, just for a few minutes. He laid back and listened to the sound of his steady breathing. He could tell he would be asleep in moments.

Or he should have been.

The loud *clatch* noise startled him in the silent room.

Exhausted as he was, he felt disoriented, and couldn't place the source of the sound. Then he heard another noise that put the first into perspective. The slow groaning creak of his room's door being opened stealthily. The first noise had been the door's latch mechanism. He groaned, thinking that Gretchen was attempting to slip into his room for some nocturnal entertainment. Normally, he welcomed her to his bed, but tonight he just needed to sleep.

He would just pretend he was already asleep. Perhaps she would go away, disappointed.

She took so long in moving to the bed that he had begun to doze again anyway. When he felt her hand brush lightly along his lower leg, he woke slightly and remembered she had come in. *Not tonight, Gretchen. Tonight you find only a man that sleeps like a log.* He kept his breathing steady and was nearly back to sleep, when her hand lightly grazed his naked chest.

The slow seduction was unlike Gretchen. Normally she would have leapt giddy into his bed and announced her presence, then verbally invited him to take her. The gentle touches were new, and he thought that perhaps she wasn't really interested. Maybe she was just feeling motherly over his injury and near-death experience.

Her fingers were gone now. *She must have left*, he thought.

When her lips softly kissed his injured shoulder, he could only moan from his half-slumber. As her hand slid down his chest to the waistline of his trousers, her lips nibbled across his collarbone to the base of his throat. He felt good, but he also felt himself drifting.

Her hands were soft and magic, like they were on both sides of his chest, gently soothing and caressing his pain away. His trousers were coming away. When had he removed his boots? The soft kisses on his neck were making him forget. His arousal was beginning, but despite that sensation, he slipped deeper into blessed sleep.

Still the gentle fingers caressed him. Still the tiny lips nipped and pecked around his upper chest and his neck. He was tempted to open his eyes, and come to full wakefulness. Their lovemaking was always spirited and passionate, fun and fulfilling. But the gentle lure of rest and the temptation of lying back and allowing her to explore him was too strong.

He fell back into the sleepy drift, soaking up the soothing sensations.

Then he felt a tiny stabbing in his upper leg. *Did she just dig her fingernail into my flesh?* He nearly opened his eyes, but the playful and reassuring caresses had returned, and he had no desire for them end. The hands worked their way slowly down his legs to his ankles, rubbing his feet, molding his flesh between constantly moving fingers. Then she was back at his upper chest and neck. Then his arms. Then his—

Fritz's mind came fully awake. His eyes were closed, but the incongruity of what he had felt had shocked him into full awareness. Somehow, Gretchen was touching his feet and kissing his neck at the same time. Now fully focused, he felt her hand on his foot, while the lips nibbled at his throat. *But, that's not possible!* Then he was filled with dread, his arousal leaving him instantly. Was it somehow both Gretchen and Anneli? His friend's wife? Fritz was a man of good humor, and he loved a party and to be a ladies man, but the one line he would never cross was to bed the woman of a close friend.

His eyes snapped open, and another surprise awaited him. There were two women in his bed, but neither was Anneli Wagner. And neither was Gretchen!

Both of the women had long dark hair, and wore gauzy white nightgowns, frayed at the ends. Each gown had a dropping V-neck that stretched all the way to its wearer's waistline. Fritz recognized the girl massaging his feet. She was a waitress at the tavern in the small village, where he had bought everyone drinks. The other woman, slightly older, now kissing her way down his chest to his navel, was looking up at him with her dark eyes making deep promises.

With each touch of her rich red lips on his stomach, his shock and surprise ebbed away, leaving only the amazing waves of pleasure. He realized he didn't care who these two raven-haired beauties were, or where they had come from. He was still tired—exhausted to the point of dropping. He tried to move a hand, to touch the woman now exploring below his navel. His hand refused to move.

His eyes felt heavy as the waitress came up from his feet to kiss his throat as the other woman had done. A groan escaped his lips. Or was that only in his mind? He tried to speak to the women, but his voice was far away. As his eyes closed once more, he felt the same pricking sting in his groin, but it felt so very good, and a warmth filled him as he drifted to sleep.

Do with me as you will, ladies. I am in your hands.

CHAPTER NINETEEN

Andreas Wagner was bone tired as he ascended the stairs to take him to Fritz's room. He had stayed behind and entertained the ladies, and then he suggested they all get to their own beds, telling Gretchen not to worry for her man. Wagner would check on Fritz before he retired to his own chambers. Although Fritz had been the one injured in the fall on the bridge, Wagner was feeling the muscle ache from his rescue with the rope, and sleep was calling to him.

Moving slowly along the long corridor, with his candlelight flickering from the breeze created by his movement down the hall, he made his way toward Fritz's room, where Petran had strangely made the bed for Fritz. Wagner found it odd that the servant had prepared their rooms so far from his own, when there were perfectly good rooms adjacent to his. Maybe the man assumed wrongly that the four friends would want space from each other. He would speak to the Count about it, or maybe just leave Petran a note asking that their lodgings be moved closer, so that they needn't traipse around the whole castle just to speak to each other.

As the light from the candle dispelled the shadows at the end of the hallway, Wagner was surprised to see a dark-haired woman leaving Fritz's room. She wore a floor-length nightgown, but it was sheer, and he could see her large breasts through it clearly. She paused and looked up at him. He recognized her right away as the waitress from the tavern in the town. He had seen her there that first night, when he had stayed in the room in

Miklos's inn. He had spotted her again while eating at the tavern, when Fritz and the others had arrived. The woman seemed not to know him, and she made no kind of greeting, before she simply turned and headed the other way, around the corner and into the darkened next hallway.

Wagner stood still in the corridor. *She must work for the Count,* he thought. *As well as for Miklos.* Either that or Fritz had arranged for her to have a clandestine meeting with him here in the castle. Wagner knew his friend's womanizing ways—at least before he had started seeing Gretchen, anyway—but he found it hard to believe the man would be so brazen as to invite village girls up to the castle. It was far more likely that Fritz would have suggested a solo night in the village after drinking at the tavern with Wagner. He would more likely have found his entertainment that way. Wagner didn't expect that kind of behavior from his friend for at least a few more weeks, when he had grown tired of the lack of conversation in the castle, and he would be frequently seeking out the tavern for drink and revelry. Wagner had seen the pattern before.

And, he reminded himself, he hadn't seen that kind of behavior at all since Fritz and Gretchen had become serious. *Are things so bad between them that he's again on the prowl?* Wagner moved past Fritz's door to the end of the corridor and looked around the corner after the waitress, but she was gone. Maybe she had a room of her own somewhere. The candle threw its shimmering light down the side hallway, but the feeble illumination could not penetrate the depths of black at the other end.

Wagner turned and headed back to Fritz's door. He paused only briefly, then smiled and thought about the waitress's large breasts. *You are amazing, Fritz.* He walked on, leaving his friend to slumber after what had surely been a good time.

He headed back to the stairs and went down to the main floor. He would pass Gretchen's room, then check in on his wife, before finally laying his head on his own pillow. They had already discussed Fritz taking a few days to mend his shoulder. So on the following day, Wagner would work alone again, this time up in the tower from which the stone had dropped that had nearly killed him.

He was paying more attention to his feet than to the corridor and the shadows ahead of him—the light his candle cast only went so far. But something moved up ahead in the dark. He caught the movement with the edge of his eye, and his head snapped up. His nerves were already frayed after the day's events, and then unexpectedly finding a stranger in the castle. He held the light out and took a few more steps into the corridor. The golden light illuminated the edge of a sheer white dressing gown coming out of a room up ahead. It was Gretchen's room. He wondered if perhaps she was looking for the kitchen again. They hadn't been all together in the castle long. She likely didn't know her way that well yet. He took two more steps toward the door and was about to speak out loud to her, asking if she needed help.

But his words died in his throat before they reached his tongue.

This woman was not Gretchen. She looked a little like the waitress, with long dark hair, and the sheer white gown, but this woman's hair was straight, where the waitress had looping curls in her tresses. This woman was slightly older, but no less stunning to look at. Her breasts were small, but between the deep V-neck of her gown and the gauzy material, nothing was left to the imagination. Her long red fingernails pulled the handle of Gretchen's door closed behind her, as she stepped out into the hallway fully.

Wagner frowned and took a step forward, intending to ask the woman her business in Gretchen's room, but the woman's head snapped up, with two quick jerks, as if she were a mechanical person, and not well maintained. Her glare fixed itself on Wagner's face, and he felt his confidence leave him in a rush. He had been willing to accost this woman, but her stare had reversed the tables, as if he were the outsider.

Then she turned and strode to the end of the hall, her long legs slipping out of the gown's full-length slits with every stride. Wagner's spell was broken and he took two quick following steps, his tongue finding words in a gush.

"Just a moment! Who are you? What are you doing here?"

The woman reached the corner of the hall and was turning it when two strange things happened. The first was a burst of wind that came from her end of the hall. The gust made his candle light flicker madly. His eyes darted down to the single flame to ensure it would not go out. He raised a hand in front of the flame to stop it flickering. When his eyes returned to the woman rounding the corner into the east wing, he took a faltering step backward.

In the flicker of the dancing light, the woman's upper torso had bent backward at the waist, almost horizontal to the floor. Her legs and abdomen were rounding the corner of the hallway, but her back made it appear she was climbing up the wall toward the ceiling. Her arms were outstretched, and her fingers were clenched into talon-like claws, pointed upward. Her long straight hair dangled down to the floor, as she jerkily moved her head back to look at Wagner with hatred in her glowing red eyes.

The flame on his candle jumped again, and his eyes darted away from the horrible insect-like posture of the woman. When he looked up again, she was gone. He raced to the corner and leapt into the next hallway, his candle flame sputtering hysterically. The east hallway was as empty as the one he had just left. He twisted violently to look behind him and found only empty hallway. He twisted around again to see if the woman had ghost-like, managed to slip around him somehow. But he was alone.

He stood rooted to the spot for moments, twisting back and forth to ensure nothing could sneak up on him from behind. The small hairs at the base of his neck felt tight and stiff. Gooseflesh the size of peas stood strong up and down his forearms. His heart was pounding so quickly he couldn't make out distinctive thumps, but rather heard and felt a steady thrum, like a string on a musical instrument plucked hard and left to vibrate.

Finally, he could move again, and he went back to Gretchen's door and looked around him once more. Then he flung the door open without knocking and went directly in. The room was dark, and Gretchen lay in her bed with the covers pulled up to her neck. She was sound asleep, and snoring softly. Wagner frowned. There was no indication in the room that the strange woman had been in here with Gretchen. He twisted in the room, his candlelight throwing up large shadows in the corners of the large space. He began to feel foolish, and as Gretchen snorted in her sleep, he stepped to the door and went out into the hall, gently pulling the large wooden portal closed.

He stood in front of her door and scowled, turning left and right in the hallway, his eyes attempting to pierce the darkness. The twisted frame of the mysterious woman lingered in his mind. *It was so...* His mind struggled for the right word. *...unnatural.* The way she had bent backward reminded him of a praying mantis, even though that wasn't quite right. The way her hands had resembled claws had been even more disconcerting. He suddenly recalled another painfully clenched figure. The thing that might have been the Count in the library. The thing that couldn't have been the Count. When he had used the flashlight, and the figure had recoiled from the light. He had forgotten that startling image, but now it sprang fresh into his mind. There was something similar about what he had seen in the library that night and what he had seen just now in the hall outside Gretchen's door.

A strange woman outside Fritz's door, then a strange woman outside Gretchen's—

He broke into a run for Anneli's room, and the candle's meager flame winked out.

He knew the way well enough, and all signs of gooseflesh had departed from his arms as he sprinted through the dark twisting hallway for his wife's room. A stripe of yellow light seeped out from under the edge of her door. He didn't stop, but threw the door wide and burst into the room.

Anneli was seated at the dressing table, running a brush through her blonde hair. She was wearing the same blue dress she'd had on at dinner, and she turned abruptly to look at him as he came barreling into the room.

The look on her face expressed concern and instant fear.

He instantly regretted his hasty action. Everything was fine, and he had alarmed her for nothing.

"It's okay, my love. I was just startled in the hallway, and I… Well, I just came to make sure you were alright." He felt foolish and shrugged his shoulders.

The look of puzzlement and fear had not left her face.

A deep dread took hold of him, and he thought that the insect-woman from the hallway might be behind him. He turned to see nothing behind him but the doorway, and quickly shut the door.

"It's nothing, Anneli. I'm sorry to have alarmed you. My imagination is getting the best of me in this huge place."

When he looked up again at his mute wife, she was walking slowly to him, and looking up at the top of his head, instead of in his eyes. She crossed the room and gently touched his face. She looked into his eyes. Her big blue eyes were sad and concerned at the same time. He was about to apologize again for his foolishness, but she took his hand and pulled his arm, leading him across the room to the dressing table where she had sat.

The light danced off a sliver cross she wore around her neck on a delicate chain. It nestled in the crook of her bosom, and he found it hard to take his eyes from the symbol as it glittered in the bright room.

At the dressing table, Anneli pushed him to stand in front of the dressing table's large oval mirror. The wood frame around it was ornately craved with swirls and curves.

In the mirror, he nearly did not recognize himself.

His shoulder-length blonde hair, and even his thick eyebrows and his lashes, had all turned a uniform, stark shade of pure white.

CHAPTER TWENTY

"I still can't believe your hair, brother." Fritz laughed as he hefted the last fallen stone from the tower into a makeshift wooden chute the men had created to get debris down to the waiting wheelbarrow. The stone tumbled and crashed down the slide, thumping and bouncing as it went, until they heard the distant thud three floors below them. It had been a week since the incident. Wagner had worked by himself for a few days while Fritz rested his shoulders, and now they had been together for three days more, but each day, Fritz still commented on his hair.

"I can't believe it myself," Wagner said, slapping at the stone dust on his clothes and thinking more of the dinner that would await them than the strange occurrences that led to all his body hair turning pure white.

The others had all been startled when they had seen Wagner's head. He had explained the apparition outside Gretchen's room and how he had been momentarily terrified. He left mention of the waitress from his story with the women, but he later asked Fritz privately about it, thinking the two strange women must be connected. But Fritz denied the visitation with the waitress. "I was sound asleep," he had told Wagner. Normally, Fritz was more than happy to boast of his female conquests, so Wagner had no reason to doubt his friend. What he had reason to begin to doubt was his mind.

First the hideous apparition that could not have been the Count in the library's darkness, then the two ghostly women—one of whom bent at odd angles. Finally, his hair turning mysteriously white. It was all too much to believe. But then he had to remind himself it wasn't only him. Fritz had seen the indentation in the courtyard floor, where a sizeable chunk of rock had barely missed sending Wagner and the wheelbarrow to their fates together. Everyone had seen the giant bat on the night Anneli and the others had arrived, and Fritz recalled how it had torn and scratched at Wagner's throat. Then there was the strange incident with Fritz nearly being knocked off the causeway.

Either Wagner was losing his mind, or the castle was somehow haunted by spectres, or possibly both. In the last few days since his hair had changed color, an event Wagner was coming to think of as *the turning*, the group of friends had seen no sight of the Count, his grumpy servant, or any serving girls in transparent gowns. It was as if the castle were deserted. The men had worked hard at clearing debris and repairing walls and roofs. They had put in long days and made great progress, somehow both understanding without verbally acknowledging it, that everyone wanted to leave the castle as soon as the work was done.

Anneli had told him in writing—her only way of directly communicating with him—that she was concerned for him. She was also worried that the stress of the place was beginning to tear Gretchen and Fritz apart. Wagner had his own ideas about why that relationship was failing, after having spoken with Fritz on the stone bridge that day, but he kept those reasons from his wife. For her part, Gretchen had been much quieter since the turning. Her gabbing had been cut to a minimum, and she often gazed quietly and smiling—as if in a happy trance—when the four gathered at the table in the kitchen to eat.

Anneli had noted to him on her small paper pad that she was grateful for the quiet but unsure of why her friend had begun to daydream so much. "Perhaps it's just this place," Wagner had offered. The castle had taken on an ominous shape in Wagner's imagination. He felt a slight unease at the thought of the place after the apparitions, and it began to feel like a heavy weight tied around his waist. He felt the burden of needing to perform the work for which the Count had hired him, but also the strain of knowing he was responsible for bringing his wife and his friends to this bleak place. There were no forms of recreation beyond reading and the conversations they held. The weather was turning, and the notion of journeying into the claustrophobic village did not appeal even to Fritz, whose relationship with Gretchen was almost certainly doomed. All of these things added up to Wagner questioning his decision to come to Transylvania and to attempt a new life here.

And there were the dreams about Britta, his deceased child.

The wasting disease, as the doctors had called it, had come on quickly, and it had ended baby Britta's life just as abruptly. His daughter had been less than a year old, and it had nearly destroyed Wagner to watch so-called men of medicine poking and prodding his baby with tools and medicines that all led to naught. In the dreams, he saw her again, in her infant pram in his former home back in Munich, before she was sick. The dream was always the same. It was night and the baby slept in the carriage, Anneli asleep in a chair nearby. The window was open and the drapes—long, thin, white shreds of tattered, nearly transparent cloth—blew halfway across the room from the strong gusts of wind fighting their way into the nursery.

Wagner would walk toward the window to close the shutters, but the wind would hold him back. Then something dark would slip into the window, like a shadow. When he tried to focus on it, its shape flowed into something else. Sometimes it appeared in the dream as a wolf with glowing red eyes. Other times, the shape dissolved like smoke and resolved into the giant bat, its eyes aglow like embers in a fireplace. Other times still, the smoke would blur, like rain on the other side of glass in a storm, and it would become the Count, although his face was that of the heinous thing in the library's dark depths, and his spine would bend backward like the woman-insect Wagner had thought he'd seen.

In all versions of the dream, the creature with the red eyes, whatever form it took, bent over Britta's sleeping form and bit the side of her neck. Blood would flow out of the small infant's veins until a pool of it lay on the floor of the room. Wagner would always be helpless to stop it, even though he knew it was coming.

He would wake to a gasp or sometimes a shriek. He would be tangled in the sheets of his bed, and covered in a cold sweat. At those times he would go to his wife's room to check on her, and finding her sound asleep, with the covers pulled up around her. He would slip into the bed beside her. She would nearly always wake and wrap her arms around him, the look in her eyes speaking of concern and a love that knew no bounds. Most nights he would fall asleep in her arms, but other times they made love—with desperation and clutching each other hard. He understood that this ritual was healing them both and finally banishing the remains of their shared grief over the loss of their daughter.

He didn't speak to Anneli about the dreams. He found it odd that they were occurring just as his relationship with his wife was being renewed. Each day he felt more and more over the loss of his child, and he had seen Anneli was finally moving past the loss as well.

But the dream would find him again each night. The result was his current exhaustion, and it was making the work at hand nearly impossible.

He shook his head to clear it, and wiped sweat from his brow with a handkerchief.

"Let's get cleaned up and eat," Fritz said.

The men swatted at their thick workman's overalls, raising a large cloud of white dust in the confines of the small room at the top of the tower. Then they began their descent. They had finished with the tower, but Wagner suggested they leave the clean-up and the disassembling of their makeshift chute for the following day. They headed down to their respective rooms, and bathed and dressed for dinner, before meeting each other again, just at the bottom of the stairs that led into the great foyer with its checked marble floor.

When they entered the kitchen, they found Anneli seated at the table, reading a small book. She looked up at the men when they approached. Her look asked a question, but Wagner did not know what she was asking. Instead, Fritz asked a question of his own.

"Where's Gretchen?"

Anneli only pointed at Wagner and shrugged.

"You thought she was with us?" Wagner said.

Anneli nodded.

"No, we haven't seen her since lunch," Fritz said. He turned around as if expecting Gretchen to be just behind them on her way into the kitchen. When he didn't find her there, he turned back to Wagner, a perplexed look on his face. "Where can she be?"

Wagner saw that Anneli was scribbling on her pad, and he stepped over to read his wife's note.

"She said she wasn't feeling well after lunch and went to take a nap," he paused in his reading aloud, as his wife finished writing. "Anneli went to find her around 3:00, but there was no answer at Gretchen's door. She thought Gretchen must be with you." Wagner looked up to his friend.

Sensing, perhaps, the same level of dread that Wagner suddenly felt, Fritz turned and headed for the door back to the foyer. Wagner quickly followed his friend. As they took the stairs, he saw that Anneli had joined them.

When they reached Gretchen's door, Anneli stepped forward, between the men and the wooden slab. She held her finger up, and the meaning was clear—she wanted to go in first, in case Gretchen was not dressed. The men stopped, as Anneli entered the room. She came back quickly and beckoned them in with a wave of her hand.

Gretchen was in her bed, the covers pulled up to her neck, as they had been the night Wagner had burst into her room. She looked sickly. Her face was covered in a sheen of sweat, but her color was drained. Her normally rosy complexion was nearly as white as Wagner's hair. None of the three friends had any medical training, but Wagner stepped forward and placed his hand gently on Gretchen's forehead, expecting her to be burning up with a fever. Instead, Gretchen's skin, wet though it was, felt cold.

When he pulled his hand back, startled at the unexpected temperature, his mind filled with unbidden thoughts of his daughter's strange wasting disease, which had manifested in precisely the same way. He glanced to his wife and saw the look of abject horror in her eyes. He knew she was thinking the same thoughts.

"What's wrong with her?" Fritz asked, taking Gretchen's hand from under the covers and holding it tightly.

When he moved her arm, the covers fell away from Gretchen's neck. Wagner saw something he had seen a dozen times in his dreams. Now he questioned himself. Had he ever seen these marks on his daughter's dying form? He couldn't remember.

Gretchen's neck had two small puncture wounds, spaced an inch and a half apart. Blood was crusted around the edge of each hole. Then a lock of her hair fell and hid the holes from view. But Wagner had seen them as clear as day.

"She's dying," he announced.

CHAPTER TWENTY-ONE

The three friends took turns caring for Gretchen over the next two days. They tried to feed her broth, but the liquid would dribble down her chin, her mouth not sucking at the fluid. Petran was left a list, asking him to bring basic medicines and a doctor. The medicines came, but no doctor, and Petran had not left a reply to the note as he sometimes did. The Count was nowhere to be seen.

Gretchen's condition did not appear to be worsening, but neither was it improving. She stayed cold and white, and sweaty. Fritz had become despondent, and the lack of his normal good cheer combined with the dire situation for Gretchen, wiped away any chance Wagner and Anneli had of remaining hopeful for Gretchen. The two had discussed the similarity of Gretchen's affliction with that of their dying baby—Anneli writing her portion of the conversation on paper for Wagner to read. It was the first time they had openly discussed baby Britta's death. Although Wagner felt them moving past their shared grief, this new chapter to the story, with Gretchen showing symptoms similar to Britta's, wasn't reducing his nightmares.

Work had pretty much ceased on the restorations as Fritz and Wagner helped Anneli care for the ailing Gretchen. One of the three of them was always by her bedside. Earlier in the afternoon the men had left Anneli with her; tonight, Fritz would stand vigil.

All thoughts of strange women in hallways had left Wagner's head. Instead, his days were filled with worry, and now the time for a decision had come. Wagner stood, leaning against the dresser in Fritz's room, as his friend paced back and forth.

"We are too remote here," Wagner said, "I fear that no doctor is coming. I've searched but can't find Petran. It's possible that he isn't even in the castle."

"That weasel!" Fritz shouted. "We should just wait in the damn kitchen in ambush for him when he comes to make the meals—he never misses one of those."

"I've considered that," Wagner said softly, trying to calm his friend with outstretched palms, "but he always knows, somehow.If he becomes suspicious, he won't come, and then we won't have any food. I'd rather the supply of food keep coming, especially as we can only get so little of it into Gretchen at each meal."

Fritz saw the reason in that. "Yes, I suppose you are right. But there must be some way we can get a doctor to her. Or her to a doctor."

"I'm going to make a trip into the village on foot to see Herr Brandt, the shopkeeper I told you about. He will know where to find a doctor, and he has little love for the Count or Petran."

"I'm not sure I can stand to just sit here and wait. Why don't I go?" Fritz was pacing back and forth again. Wagner crossed the room and sat on the edge of Fritz's bed as they made their plan.

"Henning knows me. Besides, I need you to work on our backup plan, while I'm gone."

"And what is that?" Fritz's eyes came alive at the thought that plans were now being made. His depression was vanishing at the thought of taking action.

"The narrow coach. We don't need Petran to drive it. We can drive it ourselves. If there's no doctor in that blasted village, then we take the Count's coach and get Gretchen out—as far as Dorna-Watra up north, if need be, but we get her to help. We can always apologize to the Count later and recompense him for the loss of his coach. But if we can't find that skinny ghoul to drive for us, I say we take the damned thing."

"So you need me to prepare the coach, for your return from the village?" Fritz asked, clearly liking the plan.

"Yes—actually, I'll take one of the horses bareback into town. You get the other one ready, and as soon as I'm back, if I've no doctor with me, we'll hook my horse back up to the traces and load Gretchen into the carriage." Wagner stood. With the decision made, he was ready to act. "Let's go inform Anneli, so she can get Gretchen ready for either outcome."

The men left Fritz's room in a rush and made their way down to Gretchen's room. When they stepped inside the door, Gretchen was asleep in her usual place in the bed, some of her color having returned. She looked better than she had in days, and no sweat stood on her face.

But of Anneli, there was no sign.

Anneli Wagner could not remember leaving Gretchen's side, or why she had done it. She was having a hard time thinking about anything. It was as if she were walking in a dream. She was in a room in the castle she could not place. She wasn't sure she had been here before, even though her husband had showed her the whole building.

She was in a sitting room of some sort. There were very nice plush sofas and wingback chairs. Small tables were here and there, some stacked with books, others holding crystal candelabra filled with dark red wax candles. The room had no windows, but long faded tapestries adorned most of the walls, and the far wall was covered in long velvet drapes—a deep burgundy, like the candles around the room.

She took a few steps into the room, her legs seeming to float more than walk. She hadn't made any conscious decision to move further into the strange room. She had still been wondering where she was. That she found herself moving, and that she had not made the decision to do so, was disorienting. A wave of vertigo washed over her; she felt nauseous and she thought she might lose her balance and fall over on her face. Yet her legs continued to glide across the room, bringing her toward the dark velvet drapes.

She paused in front of the thick material, as if she were unsure what to do next, but her mind was still grappling with why she was doing any of this at all. It all felt slightly off, as if she were in a dream. Then, unknown to her, her own arms had moved and grasped the curtains. She quickly flung them apart, and they slid silently on their runners.

On the other side of the curtains was another drawing room, with more sofas. It was an extension of the room she had just left. But this room had fewer candles lighting it, so the shadows crept and played at the recesses of the room. She took a half step into the room, her hands still not under her control. She stopped.

In the middle of the room stood a man.

His eyes burned like twin winter suns, the small glowing coals at the center making the whites around them glow with a misty radiance.

His dark hair fell down his forehead, and his lips were drawn tight across his face. Those lips held no expression, a crack in a wall of alabaster pale skin.

The man was dressed in a dark suit of some kind, but Anneli found it hard to look at any part of the man but his eyes. Those glowing eyes. As if they commanded her to look directly at them. She once again tried to move of her own volition and found that she could not. Something else was controlling her movements, like she was a marionette. She no longer thought she was in a dream. That feeling was wrong. It was this man's doing. Somehow, in some way, he was moving her limbs for her. She knew that, but her mind could not examine the idea, as if it were covered in slippery grease, and each time she tried to touch the thought, it slid away from her.

At the edge of her vision, she could see the space around them, and the shadows reaching out from the corners and wrapping themselves around the man, to blend into the dark shoulders of his suit. For this man, the shadows were alive.

Anneli Wagner stood transfixed by the curtains, her blue eyes glazed over and her breath coming in bursts. His eyes took up the greater portion of her vision, and she felt herself attracted to those eyes, while at the same time repulsed from them. She wanted to look away, but she also wanted to look deeper. To fall away inside the fiery pits in the center of this man's glowing orbs. She felt his desire, a tangible thing, looming and full of jagged spikes and thorns. This man—*this creature*—would devour her. It would consume her completely.

She lifted her head higher, standing as erect as possible, again, the movement not her own. As she stretched, she could feel the tiny silver cross between her breasts being pulled up from its hiding spot in her yellow evening gown, as it was tugged by the thin silver necklace.

The movement caught the man's attention and he turned his glowing coal eyes away from hers for just a second. The spell was broken.

He shrieked and recoiled from the sight of the necklace, the shadows around him moving into a dancing frenzy. His body swept back into the darkness at the far end of the room, as if a strong gale wind had just blown him aloft on its currents.

"Anneli!" someone was calling, far in the distance.

The man's eyes snapped up again, this time catching her own so forcefully, that she felt her soul wrenched inside her body. The eyes were burning now with a mixture of pain, desire, and seething anger. Farther away she heard her name being called once again.

Then the eyes snapped shut, and she felt herself released entirely from the grasp of the man's powers. Her body slumped downward to the floor. She realized that she had not been standing erect, but rather, her feet had not even been touching

Anneli Wagner stood transfixed by the curtains,
her blue eyes glazed over and her breath coming in bursts.

the ground! She had been floating off the floor by at least a few inches. Her mind was her own again, and her thoughts, feelings, and movements were completely back in her control.

She looked up from the floor to the far wall, but the shadows and the man were both gone.

"ANNELI!" Her husband was near and calling desperately for her.

Filled with an energy she had not known since before her deceased daughter's birth, she sprang to her feet and rushed back through the curtains and out of the sitting room into a hallway. Andreas was at the far end of it, and she called out to him. He whirled and came running to her. They embraced, and he pulled her away from him to look in her eyes. She saw only love and concern in his.

"Where were you?" he asked.

"I saw him," she spoke aloud.

CHAPTER TWENTY-TWO

Andreas Wagner was so stunned that his wife had used her voice that he hardly registered what she had said.

"You spoke!" His smile stretched across his face until it hurt.

"I saw him, Andreas. Count Dracula. He… He is not a good man," she said. She looked scared and confused.

"Did he hurt you? Are you alright?" Wagner was suddenly angry, his elation at his wife learning to speak forgotten, and he stepped into the room from which she had just come, looking for the Count. It was too much. All the strange occurrences, then Gretchen's sickness, and now to hear that there really was something wrong with his absentee host.

"No, no. He didn't touch me. He has left. The room is empty," she told Wagner, as he came back out into the hallway. "Still, he is very frightening. I think we should leave."

"We are just about to. Come, we need to get back to Fritz and Gretchen," he said, pulling her with him as he strode down the hallway. But she was moving faster and broke into a run for the stairs. He sped up to keep pace with her, and they both ran to Gretchen's room without another word between them.

When they reached Gretchen's chamber, Fritz was beside the bed, holding her hand. She was awake, but she looked weak. She smiled slowly when they came into the room. "Hello," she said, but it sounded as if the simple word had taken most of her energy to mutter.

"You are awake," Wagner began, some small sliver of hope returning. But then Fritz turned to look at him, and the hope was dashed. He looked grave, and the set of the man's jaw indicated that although Gretchen seemed well, she really was not. Plus, Fritz was beginning to look a little pale himself.

Anneli stepped ahead to greet Gretchen, and Fritz got up from his chair to come over to Wagner.

"We need to move. Now. She is very ill," Fritz spoke softly, so that only Wagner could hear. "I think she is trying to appear strong, but I can see it. I know her. She's still getting worse."

"I'll go now. You aren't looking well either, Fritz." Wagner patted his friend on the shoulder.

"I'm quite tired. But I need to come and get the carriage ready. Let's go."

The men raced out into the hall and down the stairs to the main foyer. They went straight to the massive front door with its dark banded wood. But when Wagner pulled at the latch, the door refused to budge. He was so used to flinging that door open, throwing some of his strength into doing so because it was heavy, that he nearly hurt himself jerking on the thing, only to not have it move an inch.

He pulled a second time.

"What is it?" Fritz asked.

"The door… It's locked. It's never been locked before." Wagner said, as he pulled out his ring of keys. He had marked several of them with colored string, so he knew which keys went where, but he had never discovered the purpose of all of them—he had more keys than he had found doors. But he also didn't know which key fit the front door to the castle. It had always been unlocked, and he had never thought to test his unmarked keys on it.

He started testing them, one at a time, as Fritz looked on impatiently.

He had twenty unmarked keys. After trying nineteen of them, and looking with despair at the last one, he recalled the door in the wine cellar. The one Petran had guarded so jealously, he now realized. *What were you hiding, you slug?* He inserted the brass key and attempted to turn it, but like with the others, it was not the correct key. *Like with the that cellar door.*

"None of them fit," he told Fritz.

"Here, let me try," Fritz snatched the ring of keys and stepped in front of Wagner at the door.

Wagner was about to suggest they try one of the other doors out of the building. Surely one of his keys would open one of the exterior doors. There were several of them. He hadn't tried any of them for some reason. He realized he hadn't ever needed to—the doors were always unlocked. But he heard footsteps behind him on the marble floor. *Anneli*, he thought. *Something must have happened with Gretchen.* But then, before he could turn his head, he realized the sound of the footstep was wrong.

When the hand clutched his shoulder from behind, it felt like it weighed a ton, and Wagner knew he was in trouble. He tried to call out to Fritz, to warn him, but there was no time.

Before he knew it, he had been grabbed, thrown, and was flying across the foyer, back first. His leg slammed into the round wooden table in the middle of the room, where his welcome letter from the Count had waited on that first day. The table flipped over, and Wagner's body flipped end over end from the impact—everything appeared to be in such slow motion, that he could see the vase tumbling from the table, its water spraying in an arc, as the flowers jettisoned like missiles.

Then Wagner's body crashed into the wall, and he slid to the floor. The impact blasted the air from his lungs, and his head was filled with a buzzing hum while his chest vibrated with sensation overload, as he desperately tried to draw a fresh breath.

But his lungs felt like they had expelled their air and then sealed themselves forever.

When the breath came, it came in a gulp, as his head arced up from the floor, like a drowning man surfacing from below the waters of a turbulent lake. He saw his attacker—*Petran*—was locked in a struggle with Fritz near the door. Petran was insanely strong. Even though Petran was a bit taller, Fritz outweighed the man by probably a hundred pounds. And Fritz knew how to hold his own in a Munich beer hall.

Both men threw punches and landed them at the same time, Fritz's fist hitting Petran's cheek, as Petran's hit Fritz in the chest. Fritz stepped into Petran's next swing and grabbed the man around the waist. He head-butted Petran and then released him. The gangly man staggered away from the fighter's embrace. Wagner struggled to his feet, his breath finally returned to him. He suspected he would be sore in the morning from the impact with the table and the wall, but right now he was buzzing with anger at Petran, and he needed to help his friend. Blood was rushing in his ears and he could hear nothing but a pounding roar. He raced across the foyer toward the giant. He bent to scoop up the fallen vase from the floor, where the thick carpet had prevented it from shattering. Petran lunged back toward Fritz and kicked out at Fritz's leg. Fritz cried out in pain, and Petran moved closer to throw a punch at Fritz's eye. Clutching his knee in pain, Fritz dodged the blow, leaning to his left and throwing up his free hand.

Wagner swung the vase, and cracked it across Petran's face and temple. The tall man stumbled back and squealed like a little girl shrieking for a lost toy. Wagner didn't know a man could make a noise like that. It managed to cut through the rush of blood in his ears, and it startled him enough that he stepped backward, bumping into Fritz.

Petran continued his deathly scream, and his body flailed around the room until he bounced off the wall behind him. His face was covered by his hands, and blood leaked between his fingers. When he pulled his hands away, Wagner could see that the vase had shattered on Petran's skull and a thin sliver of ceramic had plunged deeply into Petran's eye socket with its edges pointing directly up and down. Crimson blood actually squirted from the wound, and poured down the man's ruined visage. His lips pulled back in a snarl like a wolf, and he bared his crooked teeth as if he would come to bite Wagner.

But Wagner had had enough. "We are done with you, animal!" He took a step toward Petran, when Fritz cried out from behind him.

Wagner turned to find Fritz crouched over, and a woman on his back. The waitress in the sheer gown had crept up from behind and leapt onto Fritz's back. Her face was buried in Fritz's neck, and as he thrust a fist up at her, knocking her a glancing blow to the side of her head, she pulled her face away, pulling the flesh of Fritz's neck with her, in her mouth. His neck exploded with a red spray, and the blood dripped down her chin.

When Wagner heard a hiss from across the room, he realized that Petran and the strange waitress would not be the only enemies they would face.

CHAPTER TWENTY-THREE

The hideous woman Wagner had seen outside Gretchen's room was across the foyer. Her mouth was open, like Petran's, and she was baring her teeth. But unlike Petran, her incisors were elongated like a wolf's fangs—like the waitress with the bloody mouth had. The insect-woman was emitting the loud hissing noise, and her eyes were almost glowing red. Just like in his dreams.

Fritz swung his head backward. A gout of blood sprayed from his neck as he did so, but the back of his head connected with the teeth of the woman on his back. She launched off of him, sprawling to the floor. Wagner had been distracted by the motion, and now out of his peripheral vision he saw Petran's lean form rushing him. He dropped to a crouch and punched out, hitting the tall man in the gut hard enough to knock the air out of him. Wagner sprang to his feet, his other fist leading, and he clobbered Petran in the jaw. The man's body flew into the air and tumbled over backward like a bad acrobat.

The hissing woman was on him then, having rushed him from the side. He threw the back of his fist up, and hit her in the face. She fell away from him just as Fritz was slamming into his left shoulder, turning him around in a spin.

"Run!" he shouted, as he sprinted past Wagner. The waitress had recovered on the floor, and now she crouched there like a toad wrapped in a bloody curtain. Wagner started to follow his friend, and the woman shot from the floor like she had been launched from a cannon. Wagner dove to the floor in front of him, rolled, and landed on his back.

The waitress, her bloody fangs dripping with Fritz's blood, flew through the air right over him and crashed into the strange insect-woman, who was coming for him from the other side. Both women fell away in a tumble of limbs into Petran, tripping him up, so that he landed on his face, and drove the vase fragment further into his skull. His scream was inhuman. Wagner, wasting no time, scrambled to his feet. He chased up the stairs after Fritz. The big man clutched the torn side of his neck, holding his life's blood in by sheer force of will.

As Wagner reached the top of the stairs and looked back, he could see the women and Petran following them already. He turned and sped after Fritz, realizing that the man wasn't fleeing so much as he was racing toward Gretchen's room. If these creatures had attacked the two of them, there might be more of them setting upon the women. Wagner was glad Fritz had kept his wits about him.

Nearly to the door to the room, Wagner saw something that made his last shred of hope plummet. At the far end of the corridor, and racing toward them, was Count Dracula. All pretense at civility lost, the Count bared his own fangs—longer than those of the women. His eyes were smoldering volcanoes of rage, and his hands were clenched into deadly talons. *It is all of them*, Wagner realized. *They are all creatures.*

Fritz whipped open the door to Gretchen's room and swept in. Anneli looked up in shock at their hurried entrance. As soon as Wagner was in, Fritz slammed the door behind him and threw his weight against it. Wagner hurried to lock the door with the key on his ring that had the green bit of string— the color he had associated with Gretchen, for the color of the dress she wore the day Anneli introduced him to her. His mind could easily fix on such random things, and the ability had helped him with remembering crucial things throughout his life. The lock tumbled and Fritz sighed loudly. Both men knew the door was the only way into the room.

Gretchen was sleeping again, and Anneli stood from the chair by the bed and quickly came over to them.

"What is it?"

Fritz turned to Wagner and looked helplessly at him. He turned away and rushed to Gretchen's closet, grabbing the first piece of cloth he found, and pressed it to his savaged neck. The explanation would be up to Wagner.

"Petran has locked us inside the castle," he said. Anneli's eyes widened. "We fought with him. And the woman I saw in the hallway the night my hair turned. She was real. She was…a creature of some sort. Her teeth are long and she hissed like a snake."

Now Anneli's eyebrows raised in disbelief. "She did what?"

"There are two women. Both of them are creatures more than human," hold told her, holding her shoulders and looking directly in her eyes, so she would know how serious he was. "And it gets worse. Dracula is one of them, too."

The words came out of him in a rush, dumping the bad news on his bride like a waterfall. Then he turned to the locked door, expecting the feral creatures he had faced to burst through the door at any second. But there was no pounding on the wooden door, no heavy breathing outside of it.

Fritz had grabbed one of Gretchen's scarves from a drawer and was wrapping it around his neck, using the cloth he had found in the closet as a bandage for his neck wound. "Are there any other ways into this room?"

"No," Wagner told him. He thought again about the design of the castle, and he wondered whether there might be a secret passage that led into Gretchen's sleeping chambers. "No. Just this door. Not even a window. We are safe."

Fritz's face fell, as he came to the conclusion just before Wagner did. "Then we are trapped. All they need to do is wait," he said, nodding toward the door. "Sooner or later, we'll have to leave here, and the only way out is through that door."

"What are they?" Anneli asked. "You make them sound more like animals than people."

"I have never seen anything like them. I have no idea. But they are strong." Fritz rubbed his sore throat through the scarf.

"I know what they are," Wagner told them, as he sat at the dressing table and began absently to paw through Gretchen's laid out jewelry, his mind a thousand miles away, in the library in Munich. "I read about the folklore of this region of the mountains, before I came. The legends and myths, the stories and the old wives tales. All part of the colorful culture, I thought."

When he fell into silence, the others simply waited.

He turned to them and looked at each of them in turn before going on.

"Vampires. They drink human blood to survive. There are many legends about them in these parts, but I thought they were just foolish stories for children."

Anneli's mouth hung open in shock. Fritz sat heavily down on the side of the bed, not rousing the sleeping Gretchen. "Did you read how to stop them? Or kill them?"

"No," Wagner hung his head. "Only that they supposedly come out only at night. I've seen Petran around the castle, the few times that I've seen him, in the day. But I've only ever seen the Count after dark. The same with the women."

Fritz stood again. "Petran didn't have teeth like the others. Maybe he doesn't drink blood. We can wait until daylight and try to just get past him."

"Yes, but where do the others go after dawn?" Anneli asked.

Wagner thought maybe he knew. The room at the end of the wine cellar. He was about to say so, but a sudden croaking sound filled the room. A repeated *kack-kack* noise that sounded almost mechanical, like a badly damaged clock trying to gong on the hour and failing, the mechanism's spring attempting the motion again and again.

Fritz looked ready for another fight, despite his blood loss. Anneli was looking at the door in terror, but when Wagner looked at the door, he realized the sound was not coming from the hallway. Were they trying to get in from somewhere else? Then his eyes turned to the bed.

It was Gretchen.

She was coughing. As soon as Wagner laid his eyes on her, the noise ceased, and she laid still. Too still.

He rushed over to the bed and laid his hand on her face. Her skin was cold. He felt at the side of her neck for her pulse, but he could feel nothing. He took her wrist up and checked there, then laid his ear down on her chest to listen for her heartbeat.

When he raised his head and turned to his companions, their expressions had changed. Anneli had tears streaming down her face, but she looked angry and ready for a fight. Fritz looked lost and horrified, his mouth agape and his eyes wide.

"She's dead."

CHAPTER TWENTY-FOUR

The keening wail of Anneli's cry echoed against the cold stone walls of the room. It came from somewhere deep inside of her, making her normally soft voice several octaves deeper. And Wagner could still hear the anger there.

Fritz simply fell into a chair in the corner, his look vacant. He hardly moved, and Wagner was afraid for the man's life. His blood coated the entire front and side of his shirt now, and the man's skin had gone pale. Wagner understood some of the loss of color was from the shock of Gretchen's death, but he knew some of it was from loss of blood as well.

For himself, Andreas Wagner dealt with the death of their companion in what he felt was an odd way.

It made him sharper.

He chastised himself for thinking the unfolding events had all been in his mind. Of course it had been Dracula in the library. He should have recognized the man, and he should have left the castle immediately. He should have heeded the warnings of the villagers. *The villagers*, he thought. *They knew. Damn them, they knew what was waiting for me here in the castle.* But the recrimination and clarity brought him a new sensation: determination. He would fight these hellish creatures and he would get his friend and his wife to safety. One death was all the creatures would have, and if he could help it, the fiends would have no more of Gretchen's blood.

"We will make them pay," he said.

Fritz did not respond, but Anneli raised her head from where she had been crying at Gretchen's bedside, and looked at her husband. He saw fire in those blue eyes he loved so well, and he understood that she would tolerate no more deaths either. Something strong had arisen in her. Something hard.

"What will we do? Tell me," she said.

"We wait until dawn. The legends I read talked of vampires fearing the daylight," he replied. He remembered the oddly designed windows in the castle—how they had been shaded to prevent light from entering. Still, he thought the vampires would sleep or rest in the day. He reminded himself, again, that he had only ever seen Dracula at night. *And that is why they need Petran. He guards them while they sleep...in the wine cellar's locked room.* It was all coming together for him.

"We'll need to fight Petran, but the others should be gone with the morning light. And then we get out and make our way to the village. Herr Brandt, the Bavarian shopkeeper I mentioned, will help us to escape." Wagner went to Fritz, and pushed his hand aside to look at the man's neck wound. Fritz offered little resistance. The wound was jagged, but not too bad. Wagner had been sure the vampire waitress had pulled a flapping wall of skin away from Fritz's throat, but he saw now that most of what she must have had on her face was blood. He went to Gretchen's dressing table and pulled fresh scarves from the drawer that Fritz had left open in his haste to bind his wound. Wagner folded one into smaller and smaller squares, then placed it over Fritz's neck and used two more scarves to wrap around the man, like bandages. When he was done, he was sure that the makeshift dressing would hold, although the wrappings would probably need to be changed by morning. He checked his pocketwatch and saw they had many hours yet until the dawn.

"Fritz, help me," Wagner said, and he walked to Gretchen's body.

Fritz stood and moved to the bed, then looked at Wagner, unsure of what to do. The man looked only resigned and tired now.

"Help me to shift her to the floor. You and Anneli should sleep. I will remain on watch. When I need to rest, I'll wake you."

Anneli stood and silently took hold of the body as well, her intention clear. She would move the body to the floor with the men, a pallbearer for a woman who they all knew would receive no formal funeral in the morning as they battled their way out of the castle.

The corpse was surprisingly lightweight as they lifted Gretchen's limp form and laid her on the floor to the side of the bed. Anneli knelt on the floor and rearranged her friend's hair, and then gently stroked Gretchen's head. Fritz, his work done, moved back to his chair. "I will sleep here," he said. "Wake me when you need to be spelled."

"I'm not sure I can sleep at all," Anneli said as she stood and turned to face the door to the room, which had remained silent.

Wagner went to her and gently placed his arms around her. She held him as well, and they remained unmoving for a moment. "You should try," he said. Then softer, he told her the rest: "Fritz might not be able to take the next watch. He needs rest badly. And in a few hours, if nothing happens, I will be close to dropping."

She looked up at him, understanding and acceptance in her look. She gently kissed him, then went to the bed and stripped off the cover that had been over their dead friend. She flapped the blanket out and draped it over the body, then laid down atop the sheets on the bed.

Wagner looked to a dark wardrobe, and opened it, rummaging for another blanket. He found one, and brought it to his wife. Even if the dead woman hadn't needed to be covered for respect, it probably would be quite offputting for everyone to sleep under a cover that had warmed a dying woman hours earlier. The fresh blanket was not as thick as the one now draped on the floor, but it would do to keep the chill off.

Wagner spread the blanket over his wife, and he saw that her eyes were already closed.

Anneli Wagner awoke, and her eyes flittered a few times in the dimly lit room, before she understood where she was. The horror of the previous night came slamming home to her brain, and she sat upright.

Fritz slumbered awkwardly in the chair, and the corpse of her friend was unmoving on the floor next to her.

All of the previous night's events had truly occurred.

Anneli felt her anger flare once again. Her eyes shifted to the door to the room. Andreas was seated on the floor, facing the door. Next to him were several long wooden rods. It took her a moment to understand what they were. She glanced up at the space above her, where the poles and the canopy of Gretchen's four-poster bed should have been. Instead she was seeing the ceiling of the room, far above the bed. The slim glow from the room's sole candle made the ceiling appear further above her than she knew it to be. She glanced over to its light and saw several fresh candles on the table, next to the candelabrum. *Andreas must have found more in the wardrobe*, she thought.

She looked back to her husband and understood that he had carefully taken the canopy down, unscrewing the long wooden poles, with their intricate carving work. They would be heavy, but she could see how they would make useful weapons.

She climbed out of the bed and slowly approached Andreas, not sure if he would be awake or not. She need not have worried that he would have fallen asleep on the job.

"Dawn is still an hour away," he told her quietly, and without turning to regard her.

She stepped over to him and gently draped the blanket she had brought from the bed around his shoulders. She put her arms around him then and laid her head on his shoulder. He still did not turn.

"You were supposed to wake me," she said softly.

"I never felt tired."

"I know," she said, rubbing his back. "I know. But take some rest now, while you still can. I will wake you at dawn. Give me your pocketwatch."

He stood and stretched his neck, then gave her the watch and nodded. When he went to the bed and laid down, she knew he should have woken her at least an hour earlier. She hoped the scant amount of time would be enough for him. Then she turned to the hastily improvised armory of weapons. She could see that the eight-foot long poles had been cleverly assembled with a large screw that held them together at the midpoint— they were actually eight lengths of wood that had attached to the head and foot boards of the bed frame. She sat on the floor in the place where her husband had held vigil. She hefted one of the wooden segments, and swung it out in front of her. It was weighty, but she could manage it.

These will do.

When a hand roused him from his sleep, Andreas Wagner came grudgingly. As his mind cleared the cobwebs of the deep, dreamless sleep he'd been in, he recalled his surroundings and the dire circumstances. He was surprised to see that Fritz had wakened him and not Anneli, but a quick glance to the door showed she was standing and holding one of the posts from the bed. She was patting the improvised baton as if she meant to do some damage with it.

Fritz was looking better rested, despite his awkward bed for the night, and he had changed his own bandage, and done a better job of it than Wagner had. He had also used a sheet and more of Gretchen's scarves to create a holster on his back that held two of the bed's post segments crossed in an X, with the end of each just over his shoulders.

"What is the time?" Wagner asked.

"Just after dawn. We'll go as soon as you feel awake and ready." Fritz told him.

Wagner stood and reached to the floor to pick up one of the wooden segments. He shook his head, making the last of his sleep fade from his mind, and flexed his arms with the wooden bludgeon.

"I am ready."

He walked across the room to the door and produced the key. He glanced quickly at his wife and his friend to ensure they were prepared for what might await them. Both returned grim looks of determination.

Then he opened the door.

CHAPTER TWENTY-FIVE

The corridor was dark, but they each held a candlestick in one hand and a segment of the bed in another. The light from their candles made the shadows retreat. Wagner stepped into the corridor, with Anneli close behind him, and Fritz bringing up the rear. Fritz's candelabrum was the largest that had been in the room, and with five lit candles on it, he cast the entire corridor, end to end, into light.

The vampires were not to be seen. Not Dracula, not the female fiends. Petran was also absent. Wagner knew the man would be about, and he quickly tried to calculate where the best chokepoint in the castle might be for Petran to ambush them. There were too many ways into and out of the castle for the gangly servant to guard them all. And surely one of the keys that were yet unmarked on Wagner's ring in his trouser pocket would match up to those other exterior doorways. So Petran had to have a plan.

Where will he be? Wagner thought.

He stood motionless outside the door to Gretchen's room while the others waited wordlessly for him to decide. He strained his hearing, listening for the slightest sound. He didn't hear anything, but his senses told him something was amiss. Was he strung too tightly after the events of the previous night? They should be running for one of the doors, but his skin was crawling, and he knew running would be the wrong move. Somehow, somewhere, a trap awaited them. He would not rush into it blindly.

Wagner took a step further into the hallway and the others follows, with Fritz reaching back to slowly pull the door to Gretchen's room closed behind them. Wagner took one more step and paused, his sense of alarm jarring now.

Then he heard the shuffling noise. Just a slight scuff, like fabric whispering across stone. The sound had not come from either end of the hall. Dread washed over Wagner like a North Sea wave smacking the shore.

Then he looked up.

The ceiling to the corridor was a full twenty feet high. Along the walls, many tapestries—some faded to the point that their artwork could no longer be discerned—hung draped from near the ceiling all the way to the floor. Just above the door to Gretchen's room, right up at the ceiling, and splayed across it like spiders waiting patiently for their flies, Dracula and the two women clutched the ceiling with their long claws. All three of them bared their fangs and dropped.

It was a trap. And they had stepped right into it.

The three vampires—the two women in their torn and sheer gowns, and Dracula in his customary black suit—landed in crouches on the floor, like cats. Wagner was startled when Anneli made the first move, thrusting her wooden bed segment like a jousting lance into the chest of the nearest female, the waitress. The woman was rammed back against the wall. Fritz swung his own bed segment like a club at the other female, but she leapt back out of reach and stuck to the wall behind her, again reminding Wagner of a spider. Dracula was closest to Wagner. The Count's fangs now clearly visible in the light, Wagner wondered how he ever could have missed them before. He had spoken to the man a few times. *But always in low light*, he realized.

Dracula merely walked toward him, confident and full of menace. Wagner decided not to wait and rushed the man, his bedpost leading. When he closed the distance, Dracula swept one arm out and batted Wagner across the hall where he crashed against the wall and slumped to the floor. The Count's strength was amazing. He appeared to be a slim man, but the power behind the strike was more than Wagner would have expected from a mountain of a man. He quickly understood this would be a fight they would lose.

Anneli struck her foe repeatedly, pinning the vampire waitress against the wall. The tapestry behind her tore loose, and fell down over the two women, but Wagner's wife did not let up on her assault. Fritz and the other female were circling each other, with Fritz alternately waving the candelabrum and the bedpost.

Wagner tried to stand and found Dracula instantly in front of him again. The creature rammed Wagner against the wall a second time, and he slid to the floor. Before Wagner could realize it, the Count had moved away.

"Stop!" The Count's robust voice echoed loudly through the hallway.

Wagner looked up and saw that Dracula had extricated Anneli from her fight with the waitress. He now stood behind her, his hand clutching her throat, one long sharp fingernail pointed at the pulsing vein on the side of her neck. Fritz also saw that she was captured. He stopped moving.

"Place your weapons on the ground," Dracula commanded Fritz.

Fritz looked furious. Wagner knew the man's frustration. They had not even made it steps outside the door before losing this brief skirmish. And they would all surely die. Then Wagner saw the look in Fritz's eye. His friend knew they would die, too.

The big man slowly knelt and placed the candle tree on the floor. When he stood, the bedpost was still in his large hand.

Dracula took a step toward Fritz, pushing Anneli before him as he went. Wagner took the moment to stand, his own bedpost still in his hand. He wanted so badly to strike Dracula from behind, and free his wife from the creature's grasp.

"Drop the weapon, or she will die," the Count took another shuffling step toward Fritz, the man he perceived to be the greater fighter of the group. He was ignoring Wagner completely.

Fritz's eye darted quickly to Wagner then back to the Count. His look seemed to droop, and he stretched out his arm and dropped the bedpost on the floor. Wagner took in the whole scene, but he knew Fritz was acting. He knew the man had something else planned. Wagner cocked his bedpost back behind his shoulder, preparing to swing it as hard as he could at the back of Dracula's head.

The female vampire Fritz had been battling stepped toward him. Wagner thought she was going to collect the dropped weapon.

She never got the chance.

As soon as she was in range, Fritz's hands went up to his shoulders and the waiting handles of the bedposts he wore on his back in a crossed X. Like a gunfighter in America, Fritz drew the weapons in a smooth and blisteringly fast arc, swinging them wide and in, until the tips of both weapons crashed into either side of the female vampire's head. The sound was the deep bass drum of a marching band, and the top of the woman's skull popped up like a cork shot out of a champagne bottle. A spout of blood followed it, and Wagner saw that the blood was darker than any he had ever seen.

"Noooooooooo!" Dracula's scream was so loud it hurt Wagner's ears in the confined space. The bedpost began its swing, and Wagner stepped forward to ensure the weapon hit its target. But Dracula was gone.

Wagner saw the movement, but although his mind slowed the scene down, he understood that everything was happening as quickly as lightning. Dracula had dropped Anneli and was racing toward Fritz. Anneli was ducking down to grasp her lost bedpost. The female vampire with the shattered cranium was beginning to collapse to the ground. Fritz was kicking out with his foot, the candelabrum was suddenly skittering across the floor toward the tapestry. Wagner's swing with the makeshift bludgeon was reaching the place where Dracula had just been, but the wood hit only air. Dracula had moved from the place with lightning speed.

The swing continued, having not met its expected resistance. Wagner spun around in a complete circle, the momentum from his strike with the weapon pulling his body around, against his will. He saw that the waitress vampire had somehow gotten behind him during the fight, and she was coming for him. But the momentum of the post swung him back to the rest of the hallway again. Anneli was down on the floor grabbing for her post. The candles touched the tapestry, and it lit into a roaring flame that cast the corridor into intense brightness.

Dracula had flown across the space of the hall and grabbed Fritz by the man's head. The two of them continued down to the end of the hall in a blur. The female vampire Fritz had killed was still falling to the floor when Dracula rammed Fritz's head against the far wall at the end of the corridor. Fritz's head burst like a balloon on the first impact, but Dracula continued to smash it against the wall over and over, shrieking in anguish all the while.

The fire roared up the wall and across the carpet on the floor to ignite the fallen body of the female vampire Fritz had killed. Her gauzy gown lit instantly, and she was suddenly a wall of fire between Wagner and the Count. The thought that his friend was dead had barely had time to enter his consciousness, but the instinct to escape was alive in his brain. He lurched forward, but before he could reach Anneli to help her up from the floor, something hard struck him from behind.

Suddenly the brilliance of the fire dimmed to a dark gray.

Then to blackness.

CHAPTER TWENTY-SIX

When a dim light bled into Wagner's eyes, the first thing his mind could comprehend was that he could not move his arms and legs. His chest felt compressed, and it was difficult to breathe. There was a coppery taste in his mouth that was as thick as paste.

His eyes flickered open and closed. He tried to understand where he was. He was looking at a damp stone wall, a few inches from his eyes. The light was filtering in from above him.

He moved his head upward and saw a tube of rock stretching above him to a dark metal grate almost ten feet higher. *No. Not a grate. Bars.* He was imprisoned in a narrow tube of stone with bars at the top. He had seen this sort of thing before in other castles. An oubliette. A dungeon cell so narrow, the victim would barely be able to move in it. They normally tapered down, and some of them filled with water. An oubliette was a place to put someone you wanted to forget about. Permanently.

But he was in it incorrectly.

The victim would normally be placed feet first and vertically into the pit until wedged at the bottom. Wagner was crunched up into a ball instead, his legs bent and up by his chest. He must have simply been dropped into the hole, and his unconscious body tangled on the way down. He felt a surge of panic and fought to crush it down. That would not be the way to get out of the hole. If he jammed himself in tighter he would die here. As simple as that.

He strained his ears for sound, but only heard a faint dripping noise. It didn't sound like he was being guarded. He cautiously wiggled just his right arm, which was under him. He could move it. The arm wasn't wedged—it was just numb from having been in the same position below him for so long. He pulled his arm up to his chest and wiggled the fingers, waiting for the inevitable sensation of seamstress needles stabbing into his fingertips as the blood began to flow again.

As soon as the arm began to tingle, he pumped it up and down above his chest a few times, and in a moment, it felt relatively normal. Then he started on the other arm. He wiggled his toes in their shoes and found they had not gone to sleep as his arms had.

His shins were wedged against the wall in front of him, and his back was crushed against the curve of the wall behind him. He dared not attempt to move his legs for fear he might slide deeper into the hole before his arms were ready to take the strain of his body's weight. When his left arm was fully awake, he stretched out his arms and braced his upper chest. With a grunt of effort, he lifted, and the strain on his legs came off slightly. He slid one leg down just a bit and pressed his foot firmly against the wall, bracing again between back and leg—only this time, he was using his foot and not his shin. Then he moved the other leg, and soon it was free in the chimney of stone.

He slid his left foot up just higher than the right and took the strain with his arms again, shimmying his back up before again pressing outward with his feet. The curved stone wall was slick, wet, and cold. He found that his hands were not as good for pressing outward as his forearms were, so he used his arms and his back. As he moved higher, he found it easier to breathe, because his knees were no longer lodged into his chest.

After another shuffling upward motion, he heard approaching footsteps above him. The simple *tack tack* of leather dress shoes on stone. He stopped where he was and moved his arms to make it look like he was unintentionally wedged in. Hopefully he wouldn't appear to be much higher than he had before. The thought briefly occurred to him to try to jam his shins against the wall instead of using his feet—that was how he had been positioned when he woke—but he could possibly get stuck, and he wasn't sure in the dim light it would make much difference.

He looked up and through the dark crossed bars at the top of the oubliette. Dracula stepped to the edge and into view.

The man wore a new, clean suit, but it was as black as those Wagner had seen before. He held a large crystal goblet in his hand and sipped from it. Then he looked down the hole, and stared in Wagner's eyes.

"You can struggle all you like; you won't escape from there," the Count said. He did not sound angry. He spoke as if he were bored. "I won't feed on you, Wagner. I have something special for you."

"Where is my wife, you bastard!"

"She is safe. I won't be harming her. Just the opposite. I find her incredibly beautiful. After all, your…friend…killed one of my concubines. I'll need a replacement, won't I? But don't fret. In exchange for becoming one of my wives, she will become like me…a being capable of living forever, with the minor inconvenience of needing to drink human blood. I thought I'd let her start with yours."

Wagner stared in mute fury at the thought of Anneli being turned into a vampire and becoming the property of this thing that pretended to be a man. He said nothing.

"Yes, the need to drink blood is the worst part of my existence. But every once in a while, I get to sample a variety that is particularly delicious." He whirled the dark liquid in his goblet and stared down at Wagner. "You were too clever, Wagner. If you had just come and done your stone work, things might have been alright. But Petran tells me your were sniffing in the cellar. He never trusted you. I whipped him within an inch of his life when he dropped the stone on you from the tower. He thought I would never find out. And then you brought that man to my home." Dracula's face turned to a sneer. Wagner suddenly understood that it was Dracula that had been behind the incident on the bridge where Fritz had fallen.

"He was a clout. So I took his woman. She did not last very long, did she?" Dracula swirled the liquid again. Wagner was certain from the way it sloshed up on the sides of the goblet, and took a long time to recede into the bottom of the glass, that the liquid was blood. "But your wife, your little Anneli…she is a singularly gorgeous creature. I was really going to let you all leave here with your lives, but when I saw her that first night in the courtyard…"

The bat.

Wagner had read in the folktales that it was believed that vampires could transform themselves into animals. *Can this man really turn into a bat?* But then the attack on the bridge, and Gretchen's illness, made sense. Fritz was the one who had beaten the bat off in the courtyard that first night. A bat of that size could easily have been the culprit, and it could simply have flown off. Neither of them had been looking for an enemy in the dark overcast sky that day.

"…I couldn't take my eyes off of her. She is a wonder. Those sapphire eyes of hers… You really were a lucky man, Andreas." Dracula was still going on about the first night. "If it were not for her beauty, I might have let you all go."

"All except Gretchen," Wagner pointed out.

"Well, yes. One gets peckish from time to time. Her blood was ripe, with just a hint of lavender. But this bouquet is better. This is your man, Fritz." He took a huge gulp, allowing the blood to drip down the sides of his face from around the edges of the glass. When he pulled the glass from his mouth, the effect of the blood on his face made a garish clown's smile, but his cruel mouth remained in a thin line. "Maybe you would like some?"

Dracula tipped the goblet over, and Fritz's blood rained down on the spot where Wagner was braced. It coated the walls, and splashed on his face and chest.

"You son of a bitch! I will kill you!"

"Good luck with that, stonemason. I hate to waste a meal, but the blood will make the walls slippery, which should make climbing more difficult. Plus," he paused and listened. Wagner heard small chirping noises. "it will also bring out some friends."

Dracula turned and strode away from the hole.

Wagner heard the noises again. They were both above and below him, and they were getting louder. The noises were not chirps, but squeals. A lot of squeals.

There were rats in the bottom of the oubliette. He could hear them crawling up the rock walls toward his legs. A quick glance upward showed him a large rat crawling into the top of the oubliette through the bars. It was the size of cat, and its red eyes glowed dimly in the pale light.

From some distance away from the top of the hole, Wagner could just hear the Count's voice. "Oh, and Herr Wagner? I'll make it more entertaining as well. You don't mind a little darkness, do you?"

Then the light was extinguished. The oubliette plunged into blackness. The rats below him in the pit shrieked louder, and he could hear the scrabbling claws begin to skitter up the walls faster.

CHAPTER TWENTY-SEVEN

Wagner began to shuffle upward again in the dark. He knew the rat above him would reach him before the ones below. He just didn't know how many more might be lurking on the floor above the grate, and he had no way of knowing how many were coming up from below him. But from the sounds echoing off the narrow tube of stone, there were a lot.

He strained to hear the rat above him—the immediate threat—but all he heard were the frantic sounds below him, agitated and growing nearer. He focused on moving his body up the chute of rock. He told himself he would feel the rats crawling on his body before they started to gnaw on him. If he tried to keep one leg fairly loose at all times, he might be able to bat away the ones below him. Once he got to the grate, the problem would become how to open it.

Shuffling up and repeating the same movements, with the need to exert even more force, to prevent slipping on the already damp and now occasionally blood-slicked walls, Wagner found he could keep a lid on his mounting panic. Shuffle, expand, step up, repeat. Then something thumped in his lap hard, and he knew the rat above him had fallen—or jumped—off the grill. He pushed hard against his legs and swept at the rat with his arm. It slid across him, and he could hear it hit the wall in the dark. He felt it bounce off the wall and against the side of his leg, frantically scrabbling for a purchase, before it was gone. He could hear it shriek as it fell, and the shrill cries of the others advancing up the oubliette below him grew louder.

He braced his arms again, and resumed his shuffling upward, picking up the pace, now that he was no longer worried as much about attack from above. His arm slipped once on the slick wall, but the motion made him breathe in deeply, and his chest expanded, forcing his other limbs outward, arresting a potential fall. Another step, another shuffle.

On the next step up and shuffle, he hit his head on something and nearly lost his tension on the walls. The tube of the oubliette was slightly wider now. He realized he was at the top, and he pressed firmly with his foot, bracing his back, so he could reach above him for the metal grate. His hand hit it before he was expecting to. He grabbed the bar with one hand and used it to relieve some of the stress on his foot and back, but the oubliette was still so tight he could easily remain in the position for a while. It was the rats coming up from below, and the small amount of room he would have with his dangling leg to swing at them, that concerned him. He reached past the bars with his right hand and quickly felt around the edge of the wall for the locking mechanism on the grate. Then he berated himself for not even thinking to test it with his hands. He brought up and tightened the tension on his left leg—the leg he planned to use as a weapon when the biting started—and pushed against his back, bracing himself harder in the vertical tunnel. Then he shoved upward on the grate with both hands.

He was surprised that it moved. But it only moved an inch or two before it hit its stops.

He felt around again with his right hand and quickly found a hinge. He moved his hand to the opposite side of the grate and felt with his hand reaching through the bars. *There you are.* The gate was locked with a thick padlock. Wagner sighed. The lock was broad and it felt new—there was no tangible rust on it. He knew instantly that none of the keys in his pocket would fit the lock.

Still, he thought. He pulled his hand in through the bars and reached back to the hinges. They were metal, and were bolted down into the floor of the room above. But the stone was wet and damp, and as his fingers had brushed the stone the first time and come across a hinge, it had felt gritty. He found the hinge again in the dark, but something nudged his lower spine. *Damn.*

He could feel something trying to get up his back. A wave of revulsion swept over him, and he almost screamed. Then the anger surged back in. He released the tension on his legs, pulling on the grate with his left arm, moving his back away from the wall. The rat quickly scurried upward to fill the void between his back and the wall.

Wagner shoved hard with his feet, his back mashing the creature against the unforgiving stone. The beast's bones ripped through its body with a squelch, stabbing into his back, and showering his ass with moisture. *Dear God.* He pulled up again with his arms and the corpse fell away. His panic rose again, and he could hear a keening wail. He realized it was coming from his own mouth, and he frantically reached for the gritty stone at the hinge. *Yes!* he thought. The mortar that had been used was a concrete. He knew that only a lime mortar would suffice for such a building. The concrete would not allow the water permeability necessary for old castles. The concrete trapped the vapor and the stone was crumbling from the moisture. He dug at it with his finger, and felt the soft mortar break and crumble like clay that had not completely hardened.

He reached into his pocket and retrieved the ring of keys just as he felt something brush his legs. He violently jerked his leg away from the wall, and began to thrash with it around in the confined space. Then he lowered it and swung it in the void below him. He felt his leg hit several soft spots on the walls, and the sound of falling shrieks and squeals of surprise and anger filled the tiny chamber.

He quickly pulled his leg up again and braced himself with his feet. Then he reached up with the key ring and used one of the keys to scrape and grind at the weak stone around the metal hinge. Every few scrapes he rubbed his finger on the groove in the dark.

It's working.

Must move faster. Faster. He scraped again and again, pulling himself up to put more strength into the scraping. When enough of the stone around the hinge felt crumbled, he lowered and wedged himself tighter between the curved walls of the oubliette and shoved upward on the grate. He could feel the hinge come loose, and when he checked with his fingers, he felt the metal bolts. He braced again, and shoved hard on the grate. It moved far more than it had, but not enough for him to squeeze between the gate and the lip of the floor above him. It was probably only a few inches.

He felt another rat running up his shin and then another on his arm. He flailed wildly, feeling the creature on his arm bite him three times in quick succession before he was able to dislodge it. The one on his leg was pinned between his shin and the wall, and struggling madly to free itself. He stabbed at it with the key ring, and it bit and clawed at his hand as he struck. Then he flexed as hard as he could, and the creature ceased its movements. He pulled his leg back and the crushed rodent refused to fall away from his shin. For some reason, this last tenacious clinging in death was the thing that sent him into a mental panic. He didn't want to have to touch the damned thing and peel it off his leg. He shook violently and rubbed his legs together hoping to dislodge the rat, but it was still wrapped around him. He began punching at it again and again, forgetting to brace himself against the walls in his fit.

One hand was still clinging with all his strength to the bar of the overhead grill, as his body slid down and away from his crouched brace. He swung his dangling legs madly, smashing into the slick walls of the oubliette, feeling rats bumping him and falling on him, and crawling on him. He shrieked in crazed panic, and threw his body around the cell, swing from one arm.

After a moment, he stopped and swung to a stillness directly beneath the grate and away from the walls. He couldn't feel anything moving on him, and the only rat squeals he could hear sounded far below him. *Gone,* he thought. *They are all gone now. I've killed them all.*

Slowly his control returned, and he reigned in his scampering wits. His arm was tiring and his grip on the bar would soon be lost. Then so would he. He reached up with his right hand and grabbed the bar, taking the strain off his left. Then he pulled one leg up and planted the foot on the wall, pushing his back against the other as he had been doing all along. He raised the other leg and pressed it against the wall too. Finally wedged again, he released both hands from the bars, and rested them. He breathed slowly and smelled the dank wetness, the smell of the rats, and the metallic scent of the blood all around him—now most likely some of his own mixed with that of the rats and his murdered friend.

Far below him, the squeaks began to grow louder.

There were more rats. From the sound of it, many more. And they would be here soon.

He had lost the ring of keys in his struggling, but that wouldn't matter. He no longer had time to scrape and pick.

Enough of this Godforsaken place.

Wagner grabbed the bars with both hands and slowly walked his feet up the wall, lowering his ass into the pit, and hoping nothing would take a great chomp out of it. When only his neck was against the wall behind him, and his feet were up by the bars, he pulled himself tighter and lowered his head down. Now he hung upside down in the tube of rock, his head the first and most obvious target for the rats. His hands gripped the bars and his feet were placed against them as if he meant to rocket off the grate directly down. But he had other plans. Carefully, so he wouldn't fall, he moved one hand from the bars to the lip of stone at the top of the oubliette, then the other. He hung from the rock in his inverted position and brought his knees to his chest, moving his feet away from the bars.

Then he thrust out, crushing his feet against the bars. The grate jolted and shuddered, and he almost lost his grip. Once his balance was restored, he carefully pushed up on the grate with both feet, testing how far it moved. *Further. Maybe six inches. One hinge completely free. Not enough.* He pulled his legs in again, held his breath and thrust. The noise was tremendous, with the grate first crashing up to its limits and then slamming back down again on the stone. In the confined space, it was louder than it should have been. The rats were going insane and shrieking hysterically. Wagner tested the grate. *Still not enough.*

He pulled his legs back for another attempt, and a rat leapt onto his head.

CHAPTER TWENTY-EIGHT

Screaming his voice hoarse, and thrashing his head from side to side, Andreas Wagner developed a strength unheard of, as he repeatedly smashed his feet upward until the grate flew open into the dark room above. When it happened, it happened so suddenly, that with his thrust, his legs flew up and into the room, launching him partly out of the dungeon trap, so that he landed with his legs and pelvis on the stone floor of the room above the pit. His head was still in the tube of stone and when he tried to sit up, he smashed his forehead against the opposing wall.

The rat was no longer on his head, but every nerve in his body was screaming, and he felt coated in blood. He shimmied his way up onto the floor until he was sure he was away from the pit, then he stood in the complete darkness and put his hand out in front of him. He walked quickly in a straight line, and even with his hands extended, when he made contact with the wall—it couldn't have been more than a few feet away—it was a surprise, and he stubbed his fingers.

The rats were still shrieking their terrible calls down in the hole. He placed his hands along the wall and moved sideways as fast as he could, until he reached a door. He moved his hand down and felt for a handle. It took some time, and his panic began to grow again.

Then he found it. The latch.

He opened the door, unsure of what he would find. The room or hallway on the other side of the door was just as dark.

He reached out tentatively and his hand hit something that tinkled. He pulled the hand back, then gently reached out again. He ran his hand over the shape, recognizing it instantly.

It was a wine bottle. He ran his hand further and felt the wooden rack. He was in the wine cellar. He moved his hand along the edge of the doorframe on the other side. He was expecting to feel stone, but he felt more wooden racks instead... *Of course, this is not the locked room, it is the side room from which Petran accosted me.*

Somehow, he found it very easy to believe that Petran's room was the place where such a hellish pit existed. He could still hear the rats whining in their hole. How long until they came out after him?

He stepped into the room and slid his hand to the right, stretching out in the dark. When he felt the rough surface of the stone wall, he followed it to the mysterious locked door. He knew where he was now, and how to get out. He turned around and began to walk in the dark, his hands outstretched, as he wound his way through the labyrinth of wine racks. Soon he turned to where the doorway for the stairs was in his mind's eye. He was pleased to find it right where he imagined it to be.

Once in the stairwell, one hand on the wall, he began to run up the steps.

He tripped twice, but soon the squeaks and chittering of the rats was far behind him. He shivered. He had never been afraid of rats—or any other creatures, for that matter—but the thought of being down in that hole with the rats on him made him shudder.

The door at the top of the stairs was closed. Locked, in fact, but he was far past caring about small obstacles like locks. To bolster his confidence, he began planning ways to take his vengeance on Dracula and rescue Anneli. He hefted one booted foot and smashed the door near the lock. The wooden door burst into the kitchen so hard, it smacked against the frame at the far end of its swing. Still disconcerted from his ordeal, he was past caring whether Petran would hear him.

The kitchen was empty, but the diffuse light from the shaded windows high on the walls told him it was day still. He made his way into the room, checking the corner, and now, compulsively, the ceiling, too. He had no idea where the Count might have taken Anneli, or where the waitress might be. He hoped they were all sleeping somewhere.

He would start with Anneli's room, and then move to his own, collecting some of the masonry tools he kept there to use as weapons, should he encounter the vampires again.

When he reached Anneli's room, it was empty, but the window was open, and he heard the noise of horse hooves on the paving stones in the courtyard below. Anneli's room looked out over the courtyard—it was just above the hole in the wall where he had almost met his end by Petran's hand. He crossed to the window and remained out of view while peeking around the thick hanging curtain.

The coach was ready to go. Petran was loading a black coffin into the back of the long narrow carriage, in a compartment that looked to be under the main seating area. *Where are they taking the dead?* Wagner asked himself. With the coffin secured, Petran walked out of sight toward the castle and retuned a moment later, dragging Anneli with him. And then it all clicked into place for Wagner: It was daylight—and vampires were active only in the night. Dracula was in the coffin, he was sure of it. He didn't know where the tavern girl might be, but he knew if it was only Petran he had to contend with, he stood a chance.

He raced to the stairs and down to the main foyer. The front door stood open, but he moved quickly to a closet just inside the door, where he had been keeping several tools. The first he found was a shovel, which he grabbed. He raced to the door, preparing to smash Petran over the head. But the tall servant had already managed to get Anneli into the carriage and himself seated in the driver's seat. As Wagner came rushing out the door, the carriage was already in motion.

He sprinted after it, but Petran, in his usual style, took the carriage from a dead stop to a full gallop. The coach raced out onto the bridge and was half way to the other side of it before Wagner could even make it across the courtyard.

"Damn!" he swore to himself.

He stood panting and looking at the carriage as it receded on the other side of the bridge and then swept into the dense forest.

I'll find you, Anneli. If I have to travel to the end of the Earth, I will find you, and I will make that man pay.

Petran and the Count were gone, so the only possible threat remaining in the castle might be the waitress—and it was day, so he prayed he would be okay to run back inside and grab a few things that might aid him. He encountered no resistance inside, and he soon found himself back in the courtyard, wearing his small leather pack—the electric device and a few other small tools inside—and holding a pickax. He had a long way to go to get into the village, and Petran had taken the only horses.

Wagner set out across the natural bridge. He did not look back at the castle behind him, and planned to never set eyes on it again. He would track Petran and the carriage, find his wife, kill both Petran and the Count, and then he and Anneli would travel far from this accursed land, to Germany or beyond.

He had tried to run the whole way, but soon found himself winded. The walk felt interminably long. The last time on the road he had been in the full grip of enjoying the nature around him. This time, every dark conifer looked sinister, and the closeness of the trail, which Wagner could now see lent itself nicely to an ambush, was in no way comforting. On the positive side, he knew he could make it to town with many hours of daylight to spare, and the length of the walk gave him time to think about all he had seen. Many things changed in his mind, in light of recent events. The fire damage at the castle meant there had been battles before. The debris that had appeared to be an intentional obstacle, probably was. The strange, hindering architectural design of the castle, the wine racks in the cellar, and the bookcases in the library, most likely *were* meant to slow an intruder's passage. Dracula probably did not entertain many guests at the castle, but when he did, Wagner could now see that they were not meant to leave it.

His anger swelling with every step, Wagner realized the reasons for the villagers' hostility and xenophobia—particularly when he had told them at the tavern that he would be working for the Count. He eventually came to the edge of the small village prepared to demand the help of the townsmen. But first he would stop off to see Henning. The man was older, and the closest thing to a friend in the village he had. He might not receive physical assistance from the Bavarian, but he could at least count on honesty.

He hoped.

As usual, the clustered buildings of the village were quiet, and no one was in sight. Wagner slipped cautiously to Brandt's all-purpose store and opened the door. As soon as he did, he knew something was wrong. The place was filled with a stench unlike anything Wagner had known before. Like rotted cabbage, trash, and human waste. He moved cautiously into the gloom of the store, making his way past the twisting rows of racks cluttered with every imaginable good and a healthy dose of dust on each shelf. He crept across the floor in slow segments, looking around him and up—always up—as he went, expecting an ambush. The pickax was clutched tightly in his now sweating hands, and he had its metal head up and ready for battle.

There was nothing moving in the place, and as Wagner strained his ears for any sounds, all he could hear was his own quiet breathing. As he neared the stairs leading down to the basement and the books, the smell got stronger, and he began to suspect what he might find in the stacks.

He walked down the steps, and immediately spotted Brandt.

The rotund man was standing against the end cap of one of the bookshelves—his prized collection of books. He was not moving. He stood stiffly, and as Wagner got closer, he saw the man's eyes were opened wide, and his mouth was open as well. Blood had dripped out of his mouth and down the side of his cheek. He had been dead for some time; the blood had dried on his face and crusted to a rust-colored stain.

What filled Wagner with rage was the large metal railroad spike that had been driven into the man's forehead, where most of the blood had leaked out. The spike went through the Bavarian and into the wood of the bookcase. It was likely what was holding up the man's corpse.

The method of killing this pleasant shopkeeper spoke of hatred, not just expediency. Also, his throat did not appear to be molested. The pool of blood on the floor was wide and tacky—Wagner had just stepped into it before he stopped in horror and fury at the spike. This man was not killed by the Count.

This was Petran.

Wagner could see it. The slight downward tilt of the spike. A taller man had done this. The bruising around Brandt's throat indicated very long fingers.

Another thing for which the servant now had to answer.

Wagner turned and stormed up the stairs, walking through the stacks to something he had seen on his first visit to the shop. It was just where he remembered it. A black, Swiss service revolver, and next to it, a slightly crumpled looking box of ammunition. He threw the pickax to the floor and picked up the pistol, checking it over quickly. He knew how to shoot, but he had never held one of these Swiss pistols before. Still, he quickly figured out its mechanism, and said a silent thank you to the portly Bavarian for keeping the thing well oiled and in working condition. The shelves might be dusty, but everything on the shelves was well tended.

Wagner loaded the gun and turned to stomp out the door and across the road to the tavern.

This time, he noted the large silver cross over the door to the tavern, and understood its significance. *They knew*, he told himself. *They were hoping God would protect them.* He ran up to the door and rammed his foot out, his boot connecting with the tavern door's handle. The door flew open and Wagner stalked into the room.

"God won't protect you bastards from me."

CHAPTER TWENTY-NINE

"I hope that He will, indeed, protect me," a man at the opposite side of the room said, "and if He does not, then it will be my time, and that is all."

The old man with the long flowing white beard and hair sat in a chair facing the door, as if he were patiently waiting for something, or someone. The rest of the room was empty, with no sign of Miklos or any of his other customers. Now that Wagner looked carefully, he recalled the old man sitting in the corner on his first night in town. The man had appeared to be napping that night, but now his eyes twinkled with life and something else...curiosity?

"Where is Miklos?" Wagner asked the old man, keeping the revolver trained on him.

"They have gone. All of them. You have no enemies in this room, Herr Wagner." The man leaned back in his chair, and Wagner could see that he wore a black robe of some sort, under the all the flowing white hair.

"Who are you? How do you know me?" Wagner checked the ceiling and around the room, then moved over to the front desk to look behind it, all the while keeping the gun trained on the old man.

"Very good, sir. You remembered to check the desk and the ceiling. They like ceilings don't they? But you seem to know that now. I am going to stand up, if you will allow it. Please do not shoot me." The man stood slowly, using one hand on the flat of the tabletop to support him as he groaned to an upright posture. "To answer your questions, I am the village priest, and I know you, sir, because every man, woman, and child in this town knows your name. You had the unfortunate role of alerting us all to the fact that the castle was once again occupied by a thing of evil."

Wagner came back around the desk, keeping his eyes on the old man, but he lowered the pistol.

The priest, for his part, slowly took hold of his long white beard and raised it slowly, revealing a starched white collar at his throat, above the black tunic. Wagner noticed that a large silver cross rested on the man's chest, hanging from the beefiest chain Wagner had ever seen.

"Have you been bitten?" the priest asked, as he lowered his beard.

"What?" Wagner was shocked.

"Have you been bitten?" The priest stepped forward with a pronounced limp, but the power in his voice and his bearing made it clear which of the two of them was in charge, despite the presence of a weapon between them.

"No," Wagner said. "But another has." He was thinking of Gretchen now.

"Your wife?" The priest asked, softer this time, and with some sympathy.

"No, a friend. She was bitten, and died. Then my friend Fritz was murdered. His head crushed," Wagner took a breath to steady his nerves, then continued the tale. "Dracula put me in a hole, but I escaped."

"A hole?" the old priest asked.

"An oubliette. There were rats," Wagner told him. A wave of revulsion washed over the priest's face. Wagner knew he did not need to elaborate with the man.

"Petran loaded Dracula and my wife into a carriage and they escaped before I could get her."

The priest limped forward to inspect him. Wagner realized the reason for the man's initial question—he was still covered

with blood, some of it his. He also had small bite marks from
the rats, and he suddenly became alarmed.

"I was bitten by the rats. Are they infected with something?
Will I die from the same wasting and blood loss Gretchen did?"
Wagner looked around himself as the priest quickly examined
his injuries.

"You have much to learn, young Andreas, and we have
very little time to prepare you. You say he kept your wife alive?"
The old man moved toward the stairs leading up to the rooms,
and Wagner followed him.

"The Count? Yes. He said he would make her one of his
concubines to replace the one we killed."

The priest whirled around, his long flowing hair and beard
flying in the arc. A gleam of mischief and mirth danced in his eyes.
"You say you killed a vampire? Good. Tell me, boy. How did you
do it?"

Wagner described the incidents leading up to the battle in the
corridor. He explained that the waitress had been turned into a
vampire. The old man was not surprised. Wagner eventually lead
up to how Fritz had shattered the other vampire woman's head
with the bed posts. The old man nodded approvingly, then turned
and ascended the stairs. "You were very lucky, and your friend,
although not lucky, must have been incredibly strong. I understand
how upset you must be over his death, but you must recognize that
Fritz saved your life with his actions. He aroused the anger of the
Dracula creature, and if he had not, you might all be dead."

"Wait, Father. Where are we going? I need to catch up
with that coach. That bastard has my wife."

"Have a care with your patience, Herr Wagner. He will
not get far with your wife. To travel long distances, Dracula
must rest in soil from his homeland. He must also have
complete protection from the sun, which could kill him, if he
were directly exposed to it."

The priest continued his lecture as he ascended the stairs.
"So Dracula has many small houses and waypoints, where he

might rest safely and protected from the sun. Inns and rest stops if you will. Sometimes innocuous places, and other times hives of evil. I have spent the last few days traveling far and wide to the four points of the compass. I found his rests stops, and I destroyed them. As soon as he reaches the first, he will know what has happened, and he will return in haste back to the safety of his castle. So you see, we know exactly where he is going, and approximately when he will arrive. Your wife will be safe throughout the journey. Come."

At the top of the stairs, the priest went into a room, and Wagner followed him, then stopped dead in his tracks.

The room was full of crosses. Every wall was covered in crucifixes, from small necklaces to giant crosses the likes of which would normally be seen on an altar in a church. For that matter, one wall held what appeared to be an actual altar. The room held a small wardrobe, and a tiny bed, on which were arrayed twenty or more wooden sticks sharpened to a wicked point. It was a corner room and one window held an array of glass vials and bottles with clear liquid in them. The other window had several garlands of garlic hanging from nails above the frame. On a small table was a collection of needles, bandages, journals, quills, ink bottles, and a large wooden crossbow.

"Tell me everything," the priest said. "I will prepare you, but I warn you. The journey is not to be taken lightly. It will take some time, and the preparations will be painful."

"Show me."

Once again, the old man assured Wagner he still had a very good chance of getting his wife back, safe and unharmed. Although they had been working for hours, the priest said they still had much to do, and it would not be safe for Wagner to go into battle at night, when Dracula would be at his strongest. They would stay in the protection of the room until daylight on the following day. Wagner knew the man was right, but he struggled to suppress his fear for Anneli.

The priest had listened to the tale of Wagner's life since accepting the position at the castle, and Wagner made sure to include every suspicion and thought he had throughout the telling. The old man, whose name was Abraham, claimed he had done battle with the vampire years ago, and he told Wagner countless things the folktales had left out. Throughout their discussions, the priest blessed the bottles of ink and the needles, the crosses and the holy water. He blessed the garlic and the wooden stakes, then covered Wagner with the holy water, and made countless blessings on him.

"A vampire is a creature of the night. It might look like a man, walk and talk, but never make any mistake: it is a creature you are dealing with. It has an insatiable thirst for human blood, and it will manipulate any situation it can to get a bellyful of the crimson liquid.

"The sunlight and fire are fatal to the creatures. Any other typical way of killing a human being will be useless—your friend was exceedingly lucky with his blunt trauma tactic. A thing like a gunshot wound could not kill a vampire, and indeed, it might not even slow them down, so your pistol would be useless." The old man looked meaningfully at the pistol Wagner had kept clutched in his hand through the conversation. Now he felt silly for having it out for so long. He set it down next to him, on the bed where he sat.

"Your other major weapon is the wooden stake. Through the heart, and then once the beast appears finished, you remove the head." Abraham paused to ensure that Wagner had absorbed the information.

The priest was nearly finished preparing his body with his tools. The man had not lied. It had been painful. But Wagner could see the art to it, and understood how all the information and preparation would help him in the coming battle. They had been in the room for hours, with Wagner learning all he could from Abraham on ways to kill a vampire, and how they thought and acted. Many of his own observations about the tactical nature of the castle had been confirmed.

Abraham had remained in the village after he had thought Dracula dead, all the while keeping an eye on things and hoping never to have to impart his knowledge to another before he died. He, too, it seemed, had suffered an incredible fright that had turned the last of his hair white, and Wagner could see from the animation in the man's face as he spoke authoritatively on the subject of vampires, that Abraham was a far younger man than Wagner had initially thought. Surely no older than sixty, yet with the long flowing white hair, the man could have easily passed for an octogenarian. Unfortunately, the man had a limp, and he would only slow Wagner down. The priest didn't offer to come with him, but it was understood he would have been a physical liability had he done so.

"I am sending you at dawn with this bandolier of pouches." The old man showed the leather sling to Wagner. "It contains garlic, several small crosses, and these spheres of glass filled with holy water. You can use them like grenades. Remember to keep Dracula and his female vampire at a distance as much as possible. If they get in close, their strength and speed could be the end of you. Do you understand?"

"Distance fighting, yes." Wagner nodded.

"One other thing, Andreas. Your friend, Gretchen, was it? You understand that Dracula might have turned her?"

Wagner looked up at Abraham in surprise.

"She might rise as one of them. It is unpleasant, but it is a possibility. If you see her and she is anything other than a deteriorating corpse, you must assume she has been turned." Abraham stopped what he was doing, packing small vials into the last pouch on the bandolier. "If she has turned, you must understand that she is no longer the friend you once knew. She is now an animal. A beast, no different from an African lion or a wolf in the forest. She exists now only to murder

you and drink every last drop of your blood. You must forget
what she looks like, and dispatch her, as I have shown you.
She will be a thing only, no longer human. You will not be
murdering her, only stopping abuse of her corpse by this
fiendish condition of demonic animation. You will be doing
her memory a favor." The older man paused again, looking
Wagner in the eye to ensure comprehension.

"Your most trusted allies will be these crucifixes and your faith
in the almighty. You will be able to hold Dracula at bay with just the
sight of the cross. I'm giving you several. Try not to lose them. Be
quick, be violent, be sure. The water will burn them like the
sunlight. Treat the crypt as I described earlier, and if you can find
your wife and get out without battle, it might be the better part of
valor. But I would prefer you put the beasts down for good. Should
you catch them sleeping, do it fast and efficiently.

"Most of all, you will need to watch out for the manservant.
He will most assuredly be awake and waiting for you. Think on
your knowledge of the castle, imagine where he might lie in wait
and where he might set traps for you. On him, you should use
your revolver. He is still human, and will die like any other man.
Find him first, and kill him, or you won't stand a chance with
Dracula or the woman. Petran will guard them with his life, like a
dog. More than just fearing his master, he hungers for the
immortality the vampires possess, and he will do whatever he
needs to do to ensure that the Count will eventually reward him."

"Will he?" Wagner asked curiously. He thought with the
way Dracula treated Petran there was no way the Count would
eventually elevate the man to the status of a vampire.

"No, because you will kill them all in the next eighteen
hours," Abraham spoke loudly, with force, as if reminding
Wagner that his duty was somehow sacred. "But if not, would
Dracula eventually turn Petran? No. Unlikely. He is a sad,
deluded fool, and Dracula will use him and spit him out when
the man is no longer of use. Then he would simply lure another
feeble mind to do his bidding."

As dawn approached, the old man fell silent, having said all he needed to say. He had instructed Wagner with all he would need. Wagner picked up the leather bandolier with the pouches, and began arming himself with crosses and wooden stakes, strapping them on to his legs with bandages. When he was ready, he faced the priest. They quietly appraised each other for just a moment, then Wagner turned to the door, ready to hike back up to the castle as soon as light pierced the sky. He descended the stairs to the main tavern, and the priest followed him.

"Take the horse in the inn's stable. She will let you ride her like lightning. Be swift. Every moment wasted is a moment closer to sunset and death." The priest held his hand out to shake Wagner's hand. Wagner took the firm grasp. The old man did not let go. He looked solemn and sad.

"Andreas…if for some reason you are too late…if he has turned your wife, you must treat her as the others."

Wagner's head jerked up and he stared into the old man's eyes.

"Andreas, you *must*! With no remorse. Remember, if he has turned her into a vampire, then she is dead, and the thing inside her body is defiling it. Treat it with the same hatred you would have for a man you found urinating on your mother's grave. The vampire is a defiler of life, nothing more."

Wagner pulled his hand away, and frowned. "If he has turned her, I will kill her. And him. And I'll burn this entire country to the ground."

CHAPTER THIRTY

The sun was obscured behind a thick vein of muting cloud cover. Wagner found the brown mare in the barn behind the inn. She was amiable enough. After she munched an apple Wagner gave her, he saddled her and swept up into the smooth leather. He didn't know the horse's name, but he whispered to her of his need to reach the castle swiftly. The horse appeared to understand and quickly sped to a gallop. They rode through the fields and woods in silence, Wagner gently stroking the creature's neck with one hand, hardly needing to use the reins at all. The animal knew the way.

He left the horse in the forest on the other side of the natural bridge, certain if he brought her to the door of the castle, he would find her dead when he eventually emerged from the inside. He approached the castle's courtyard with caution, scanning the upper reaches of the structure for signs that Petran might again attempt to crush him with falling rock. He saw no movement, and nothing to indicate that the castle might be occupied at all. He could move around to the stables to see if the carriage was back, but he did not want to waste the time.

He had stopped on the way out of the village for one more item he had spotted in Brandt's store, which his subconscious had registered—a lock-picking set. The stench in the small shop had grown, and Wagner felt a pang of guilt that he could not spare the time to take the his friend's corpse off the spike and give him a proper burial. A task for after. Despite the smell, the stop at the shop was well worth it. Wagner did not know what kind of obstructions and defenses Dracula and Petran might have left to guard against his incursion, but he knew the simplest would be just to lock the front door.

He approached the building, still wary of danger from all sides, and reached for the front door's brass handle. The door opened without hindrance, and swung smoothly with no sound. *No, of course, the fight will be inside, where they have the advantage.* He moved into the foyer, with the pistol at the ready. The crossbow was strung across his back, and he could get to it quickly. The string was taut, but the bolts were in a pouch on his hip. He didn't want to accidentally shoot himself in the head. Either weapon would do for Petran. The stakes were for Dracula and the woman.

And possibly for Gretchen.

He crept across the foyer, his eyes darting to the ceiling, the doorways, and the balcony up above.

No movement.

He didn't know where Petran would be waiting for him, but he knew the surest way to get the man's attention would be to head down to the cellar—to Petran's room with the oubliette and the locked room he assumed to be the Count's resting place. The priest had told him that Dracula would likely rest in a coffin or a stone sarcophagus in the most protected part of the castle. From that information, it was easy enough for Wagner to deduce where the Count liked to sleep.

He walked down the corridor to the kitchen, intending to go directly to the stone spiral stair. As he entered the room, gun first, something flew across the room, hitting his hand and knocking the gun from his grasp. The gun launched across the room, and skittered under a heavy stove. His hand stung and vibrated from the impact, and the object that had hit him clattered to the floor at his feet—a heavy fry pan.

He quickly stepped back into the cover of the hall and unslung the crossbow from his back. Petran rounded the corner at a run, swinging a large ax at him, the man's ruined eye now covered with a black leather eye-patch. Wagner managed to get the unloaded crossbow up just in time to deflect the blow. Even still, the force of the strike sent him staggering back several steps into the corridor. He had to remember that Petran was far stronger and much taller than him. His swings with a weapon like an ax could be devastating. Still wearing his dark blood-covered suit from their last battle, the servant grunted and took a step forward, preparing to swing the ax laterally.

Wagner rushed inside the swinging arc of the handle of the ax, and shoved the tip of the strung crossbow up under Petran's chin, pushing the man's head up and forcing him back a step. Wagner decided to take a gamble. If Petran was motivated by seeking eternal life, then maybe the thought of losing his life now would cause him to hesitate.

"Stop now, Petran, or I shoot!" Wagner shouted, and he hoped that the servant had not had time to notice the lack of a bolt in the weapon.

Petran's eyes were crazy and glazed. For a second, Wagner thought the man would continue to fight. But he stopped, dropped the ax to the floor, and tried to step backward. Wagner stepped forward, keeping the crossbow vertical under Petran's chin, where he'd be less likely to see it wasn't loaded.

They crossed into the kitchen, the tall gangly Petran backpedaling, and Wagner advancing to keep pace. Petran's face was filled with a malevolent hate, his mouth dripping saliva from the corners and his lone eye squinted, over sneering cheeks and lips. He began to move his hand upward and Wagner jabbed him hard again in the throat with the wooden top of the crossbow.

"Where is he? Down in the cellar, yes?" Wagner could see the recognition of the truth in the man's face, even had he shook his head no. "And where is my wife?"

Petran did not answer that one. Instead he quickly reached up and shoved his hand inside the string of the crossbow, attempting to hold the string back. Wagner rammed upward on the stock of the device, smashing it hard into Petran's jaw. The man stumbled backward, but did not release his hold on the weapon and it flew from Wagner's grip.

The crossbow fell to the floor, as Petran stumbled backward after hitting his leg into a table. "Not even loaded…" Petran's fury made the words come out in a spitting slurry. He bent down and grabbed the table and lifted it.

Wagner turned and launched himself back to the entrance of the corridor, just as Petran heaved the table across the kitchen. Wagner darted into the hallway and dove toward to floor. The table smashed into the corner, just as he passed it, but it still crushed his booted foot against the wall. A rocket of pain launched up his leg, even as he fell to the floor.

His foot hurt, but he tried to ignore it and focused on his hands. They would save his life in the next few seconds. His foot could be dealt with later. He stretched out and grabbed the handle of the ax Petran had dropped. The table had broken when it hit the wall, and pieces of it were scattered around the mouth of the hallway. Wagner struggled to his feet, leaning on a broken portion of the table and one of its legs as he did so. Then he pulled the ax back and swung it at the doorframe, even before Petran came into sight.

Halfway through the arc of the ax, Petran appeared with a large cooking knife in hand. The swing was good, and the ax took the man's arm off at the upper arm. It fell to the ground with the knife. Petran kept coming, as yet not even realizing he lost the arm. Wagner was surprised to see very little blood from the initial slice. It was as if the blood hadn't yet realized it was free to spurt out. Petran rammed into him, sending them both careening down the hallway in a tumble of bodies, limbs, and blood.

Wagner sat up from the floor, but Petran crashed his forehead into Wagner's face, smashing him back against the floor. His vision went blurry for a second, and then Petran's remaining long fingers were around his throat, lifting him, and sliding his back horizontally along the wall, as the man's severed arm sprayed blood behind him.

From where they struggled at the end of the corridor, Petran shoved with his remaining hand, and Wagner's limp body flew out into the foyer to tumble in a heap on the edge of the checkered marble floor. He groaned and tried to stand. He found he couldn't.

Petran stalked toward him, howling in pain as blood gusted out of his stump. Wagner looked down at himself. He was wet all over his chest, but there was very little blood. *Ah, the holy water*. He reached down to his leg, and pulled one of the wooden stakes from the sheath on his thigh. He was lucky none of the sharpened sticks had punctured his own leg in the skirmish.

Petran was on him again, the man's long, gangly fingers fully wrapped around Wagner's throat and drawing him up into the air again. Wagner swung the stake overhand, plunging it into Petran's sole remaining eye. The man howled and dropped Wagner, then dropped to his knees, the foreign object lodged firmly in his eye socket. Wagner wasted no time scrambling to his feet, then kicked out as hard as he could with a booted foot. He drove the wooden stake deeper into Petran's head, and through his brain. The shrieking ended immediately, and the tall man fell over backwards to the floor.

Wagner slumped back onto the carpet. He was exhausted from the fight, even though it had been brief. If only he could rest, just a bit before he needed to go on, he thought he might be alright.

But he heard a strange whistling noise, low and long, like an old dark melody or a dirge. When he looked up to the corridor leading to the kitchen, he saw the waitress vampire. She still wore her tattered gauzy gown, and he could see her full bosom under the sheer fabric. It was open nearly to the waist in front, and her dark ringlets of hair draped down her shoulders. She was terrible and beautiful in equal measures.

She was whistling slowly as she walked into the foyer, unconcerned at the sight of the blood around the room, or the dead servant in front of Wagner. Her eyes narrowed, as she glanced from the body to Wagner and back again to the body, as if she could not decide which she wanted to suck dry more.

"It's time to die now, dearie." She said, her voice a high croaking sound, nothing like it was when she had been alive and serving him his food at the inn. She rushed at Wagner.

He reached for his chest pouches, feeling one of the few remaining pouches that still contained bulging objects. He pulled out the head of garlic, and threw it at her across the room. She flinched, but the garlic went wide and rolled away across the floor. She was on him in a second, her long nails digging into the sides of his throat as she hoisted him to his feet with supernatural ease. Her mouth opened wider than a mouth should, showing her long fangs, as they made their descent toward his neck.

CHAPTER THIRTY-ONE

Dangling from his throat, the air cut off from his lungs, Wagner's fingers scrambled at the pouches hoping to find one last head of garlic. He found a round bulge in one of the remaining leather pockets. The outside of the bandolier was wet from the shattered vials of holy water, but he was able to work two fingers inside the flap. The she-creature was descending on his throat to suck the life from him, and spots of brilliant purple and deepest black were forming around the sides of his vision.

The garlic felt unusually slick in his hand. Then he realized it wasn't the skin of a garlic bulb his fingers were touching, but smooth glass. One of the bulbs of blown glass remained. He tightened his fingers around the thing and yanked it from the pouch, raising his hand up, and stuffing the liquid-filled globe into the vampiress's open maw.

Her instinct—the instinct of all vampires—was to bite down.

Her fangs pierced the glass, and it exploded in her mouth and throat. Instantly, Wagner felt the tension on his neck lessen and then disappear. A great welling cloud of steam like the smoke of acid burning its way through metal boiled out of her mouth and lifted toward the room's vast ceiling. The creature threw its head back and the clouds of steam now shooting from her throat filled the room. This close to her, Wagner could see the great angry red boils and pustules forming on the vampire's neck and face as the holy water did its work. Blood began to leak from her eyes and her ears, and then her eyes shriveled to black nuts and fell away inside her head. As her body collapsed to the floor, the space around Wagner was filled with a deep burning stench, like rich dung in a campfire. Wagner watched as her facial skin shifted and began to slide off her face.

When she hit the hard, unforgiving floor, her skull was nearly clean of hair and bone.

Gooseflesh broke out on Wagner's skin as he watched the woman's body continue to move and gyrate on the floor. Quickly he withdrew one of the few stakes he still had on him and plunged the thing into her heart. The blood that welled up from the sides of the puncture looked black and thick to the point of being jelly. Finally, she stopped moving, and Wagner sank back on his heels and sighed in relief.

He sat on the floor for just a minute, his eyes constantly roving between the dead vampire, the dead servant, and the doors.

Before he knew it, he was looking at the ceiling, and the smoke swirling around it. The white mist was calming and he took a few deep breaths to steady his nerves further, before he would sit up.

When he opened his eyes and lifted his head from the floor, the room was dim. Not dark, but dimmer than it had been in the early morning. He sat and looked at his watch. It was late in the afternoon. Not sunset, but close to it. He had fallen asleep. He groaned.

Then he stood and shambled down the corridor to the lost ax. He was limping slightly, but he realized he foot was not broken from the impact with the table. When he returned to the foyer, he took two swipes with the ax to sever the freakish skull with the long fangs from the vampiress's unmoving mass. Only then did he retrieve his stake from her. For good measure, he removed Petran's head with the ax as well. The servant's long neck was easier to hit, and Wagner took the head off in one clean swipe with the ax. He then retrieved the wooden stake from Petran's skull. He had to put his foot on the skull to hold it steady, and pull with most of his strength to free the deadly implement. It came loose with a sluicing sound that made his stomach flip.

He sheathed the stakes on his leg, and then quickly walked around the room, collecting the weapons he had lost in the battles with Petran and the female vampire. The rest of the holy water was gone—the unused ampules having shattered inside their nesting leather pouches on the bandolier. He still had a few heads of garlic, though for the life of him he couldn't understand why he wasn't able to lay hand on them when he had needed them. He shifted them to the central pouches where they would be easier to reach, and delicately removed the shards of broken glass so he would not slice his fingers apart when reaching for the garlic. He still had a small metal flask, which had fit in a hip pocket—the last of his holy water, and reserved not for battle, but for another purpose. He collected the unused stakes that had fallen from their sheaths, and the bolts for the crossbow.

When he got to retrieving the crossbow in the kitchen, he saw that it was beyond salvage. The string was snapped, and the wooden cross lath was shattered. He briefly considered trying to splinter the device further, to use as a makeshift stake, but decided he had enough stakes with the four he had. He had somehow lost the large cross; he quickly skimmed his surroundings, to no avail. He then broke a small piece of the table to hold horizontally in his hand with a stake crossing it vertically, forming a makeshift cross. He still had the small necklace cross from one of the pouches on his bandolier, and he donned that around his neck.

Finally, he took the ax. There would be more beheadings in his immediate future.

Limping, he took a candelabrum and lit all five sticks with matches from a nearby shelf, then made for the door in the kitchen that led down the spiral steps to the wine cellar…

…and to Dracula.

He didn't expect any resistance on the stairs, but he still took them cautiously, now ascribing a far more calculating and venomous nature to Petran than the man might have been capable of. He looked for traps and thought about the rooms off the stairs before the cellar, and what might await him in them. But he encountered no troubles, and saw no signs of Dracula or any other vampires.

By the time he reached the bottom of the stairs, the soreness in his ankle had subsided a bit. He maneuvered through the wine racks to the locked door and set the candelabrum down on the floor. He pulled out the lock picks. One of the tools was bent in the scuffle upstairs, and he spent precious minutes straightening it against the stone wall with his hand. Then he went to work on the lock on the door, and found it surprisingly easy to open. He put the tools away and quickly checked the side door behind the wine rack to the oubliette room, relieved to find that it was still closed. He stepped back to the door he had just unlocked, and slowly opened it with one hand, the ax held aloft in his other.

The door swung open and the ocher light from the candles invaded the darkness, showing Wagner a raised stone sarcophagus in the center of the space, its head toward the door. The lid was pushed slightly off the side, as if someone had been peeking into the box. Or out of it.

He retrieved the candelabrum, and checked the ceiling and around the room. In the far corner was another small door, only a few feet high—surely used for storage more than for people. When he took a second to think about what kind of storage, his stomach roiled. *Probably another vampire sleeps in there*, he thought. He set the ax down against the wall, then pulled out his stake-cross. He peered into the open stone coffin, and found that it was empty. He quickly looked around the room again, and reassured himself that he was still alone. The priest had prepared him for this eventuality, and he knew what he needed to do. Even though every bone in his body bade him to hunt through every room of the castle for his wife, he needed to finish in this dark crypt first. He set the candle tree down on the foot of the stone coffin lid, and cross-stake in one hand, he went over to the small door, and flung it open.

He was ready to stab with the wooden stake. Ready to plunge the tip into a vampire's heart or to be greeted with a disgusting pile of human organs and vats of blood. He was not expecting what he found. The small crawlspace was filled with glinting golden coins that washed out into the chamber like a cascade. He tentatively picked one up and examined it in the light. This was where the Count's great source of wealth was—how he was able to afford expert stonemasons and all the books. But the gold did not interest Wagner at the moment, at all. He had work to do.

He stood and walked back around the raised coffin and peered into its empty depths where the lid had been slid aside. The cross-stake held tightly in one hand, he withdrew the remaining heads of garlic with the other. He tossed one of them into the coffin, so it would roll to the bottom, as Father Abraham had instructed him. He took the second and crushed it in his hand as best he could, rolling it apart and dropping bits into the head of the coffin. Then he withdrew the flask. He glanced around him at the door to the room, then turned back to the sarcophagus. Wagner prepared to defile Dracula's crypt with the holy water, as something just as dangerous slinked up behind him.

He was just about to dump the liquid from the flask into Dracula's resting place, when he heard the soft whisper of fabric on skin behind him. He whirled, stake at the ready, but was unprepared for what he found.

Gretchen looked lovelier in death than she had ever looked in life. Wagner almost didn't recognize her. Her hair was straighter, and her breasts, while still attractive, no longer looked like overripe melons stuffed into her brassiere. She wore a simple gown, cut low in the front, and she walked toward him

Wagner prepared to defile Dracula's crypt with the holy water,
as something just as dangerous slinked up behind him.

slowly, gyrating her hips as she moved. She swayed like a snake, and he found the movements mesmerizing. She was looking at him with what seemed to be both need and uncertainty in her eyes. For a second, he allowed himself to believe they had all been wrong—Gretchen had awoken from her illness, and now she was confused and needed his help. Her eyes were dark in the feeble light, and she approached him as if she knew him.

"Andreas?" she asked, like a lost, scared child. "Where is everyone? What is happening?"

He was speechless, and his mouth hung limply. He watched her face now, looking for something—a sign—that he should move, that he should react. But all he felt was tired. He wanted to tell her everything would be alright. She stepped up to him and put her arms around him, clearly needing comfort. He put his arms around her back, and prepared to tell her everything would be fine.

But he noticed his hands were empty. No holy water flask, no stake or makeshift cross. He didn't know when or how he had dropped the items. But the priest's words came haunting into his memory: *She will be a thing only, no longer human.* His left arm tight around her lower back, his right hand slipped lower and grazed his thigh, just as he heard the strange creaking in her jaw, as she opened her mouth wide and tilted her head up to him.

"Not a drop," he told her, as he thrust a stake into her back, piercing her heart, and jabbing the sharpened tip out through her rib cage to press against his own chest. Her mouth froze in its wide open position, droplets of saliva glistening on the tips of her long fangs. *Not human,* he told himself. *I'm doing her corpse a favor.* He let the grotesque thing that used to be his wife's friend—his friend—fall to the stone floor, and berated himself for feeling attraction to her, for being unfaithful in his thoughts to his wife, and for wavering, for even a second, in his duty to kill the thing.

Then he felt his anger rising again. *He did this. Dracula.*

He bent down to scoop up the flask, and swiftly emptied the contents, some of which had spilled to the floor, directly into the open coffin. A haze of smoke filled the space. Wagner kicked hard at the lid with his foot. The stone cover scraped off to the side and hit the floor with a rumbling boom. The mist-like smoke from the holy water he had poured into the sarcophagus refused to leave the stone container, floating around in it like it was at home. *Good*, he thought.

He grabbed his ax and went to work on the Gretchen-thing's head. Once it was free, he collected his stakes, and filling with an intense burning hatred, he made a solemn vow.

"You will be avenged, Gretchen. Dracula is next, and he will never create another."

CHAPTER THIRTY-TWO

Wagner stormed up the spiral stairs, ideas formulating in his head with each step. Ways to stop Dracula, and ways to make him pay if he had hurt Anneli—or God forbid, if he had already turned her. Armed now only with the ax, his stakes back in their sheathes, the candelabrum, and one final head of garlic, he continued up the steps, and out into the kitchen. He had no fear that Dracula would somehow get behind him now and seek refuge in the cellar. Following the priest's instructions, he had made the sarcophagus uninhabitable to a vampire. He expected the Count would prefer to fight instead of hide anyway.

When mocking laughter rang out and echoed around the hallways and rooms of the giant castle, Wagner knew his instinct about the creature was correct. He didn't know how to find Dracula, but an idea that was born of vengeance on the stairs now became a stratagem of battle tactic. He knew how to draw the wily vampire out of hiding. Wagner quickly searched the kitchen, finding rags, bottles, and cooking fuel oil, each of which stuffed into or through his bandolier.

He mounted the main staircase, whistling loudly. As he got closer to his intended target, he began talking, trusting that if Dracula could not yet hear him, then the Count would at least make an appearance quite soon.

"No more games, Dracula. I know how to get you to come out of the shadows."

As he spoke, Wagner stepped into the darkness of the library. Setting the ax and the candelabrum down, he took one of the bottles with the oil in it, and stuffed a small strip of fabric into the neck of the bottle. He lit the end of the strip of fabric with a match, which illuminated the space around him. Then, nearly anathema to his being, he hurled the makeshift bomb at the far wall of books. When the glass exploded, the fuel oil and its vapors and droplets in the air caught fire with a loud thump. Then the flames leapt at the wall, clawing and scratching their way up toward the high ceiling, like rabid animals. The old and brittle spines of the books and the glue and string that bound them, caught alight and spread. The room was thrust into near daylight, and the blaze showed no signs of stopping.

"I am going to remove the shadows. I will set the whole damned building on fire, Count. You won't escape me, I—"

Wagner was cut off as something slammed into him from the side, sending the next bottle of oil with its freshly lit fuse tumbling from his hands. It shattered on the floor, spraying its liquid across the room, and flames lurched out of the puddle as if it were a hole through the floor of the library directly into Hell itself.

The Count had burst into the room, throwing Wagner aside. He looked frantic, like a man hoping beyond all reason to save his beloved library—just as Wagner might have been if the library had been his. It hurt his heart to set the room on fire, but his plans were to destroy the castle, after he had killed Dracula—a small price to pay for the deaths of friends. He staggered to his feet, while the Count recoiled from gouts of flame that jumped across the room. The Count was desperately looking around for something with which he could douse the blaze, his long black cape fluttering behind him. Had the fire been smaller, Wagner thought the cape might have done the job, but the flames were crawling to the ceiling of the vast library now, and soon the entire castle—or the parts of it that would burn—would be alight.

Wagner picked up his ax, and held his stake vertically, with the small cross-bar piece of wood he had picked up. He stepped up behind the Count. The man's dark suit and cape were covered already in the falling gray ash, as case after case of books and rare manuscripts went up in a rush of flames.

"Noooo! What have you done, you mad German?" Dracula whirled on Wagner and leapt for him.

Wagner raised the makeshift cross and shouted at the creature.

"Back!"

Dracula recoiled across the room, deathly afraid of the holy symbol. He turned and fled into a corner, to a door Wagner had not seen on his earlier visits to the library. Wagner pursued the Count. He stepped through the door and into a small drawing room, with a curtained entryway into yet another sitting room with plush furniture. The thought flitted through Wagner's head that all the rich fabrics and tapestries in the room would catch fire as easily as the books in the library.

The Count was somehow gone. Wagner checked the ceiling, then was about to look behind the curtains bisecting the double lounge when he heard the noise behind him. Dracula was on the wall above the door he'd just come through, but he had no time to turn before the creature had leapt and landed on his shoulders, crushing him down to the floor. The ax flew from his hand and slid across the rich carpet, well out of his grasp.

But then the Count was up and running for the door at the far end of the room. Wagner stumbled to his feet and saw just the tip of the Count's cape disappearing through the door. He ran across the room to catch up with the creature. If he let Dracula escape, there were countless places in the castle he could hide. The wooden inner structures of the building might collapse before Wagner could find Anneli. He had to keep up.

As Wagner came through the door, something was flying for him. He ducked back into the doorway in time to avoid a hurtling vase, which shattered against the door frame. When he looked around the frame again, Dracula was far down the hallway. Wagner raced after him.

"There's no escape Count," Wagner called after him. "All your resting places around the countryside have been destroyed. You're trapped here in your own burning castle!"

"Impossible!" the creature called out from the shadows. With the candelabrum left behind and the glow from the flames in the library receding, Wagner was finding it harder to see.

"I will find a way, Wagner. I have for centuries now," Dracula called, his voice echoing oddly in the twisting corridors of black. Sometimes near and sometimes far. Wagner could not determine the Count's direction. "You think you are special?" The voice was far away. "That you, and you alone, can stop me?" Now the voice was so close, Wagner whirled in the dark, thinking the vampire was right behind him. But he was alone.

He pulled his small leather pack off of his back and withdrew an object from it, holding the item at the ready. He felt the attack was coming.

"With your pitiful wooden stakes and crosses. You have nothing that can defeat me. I am invincible...I am the night...I am—"

Dracula was right behind him. Wagner whirled and activated the flashlight. The vampire recoiled in horror as if the tungsten light was a beam from the sun itself. He retreated from Wagner and smashed into the hallway's wall just feet away.

"...bruised?" Wagner asked with a malicious grin. He hurled the last head of garlic at the creature, and it bounced off of the vampire's forehead, leaving a hissing, smoking scorch mark as it ricocheted, "...a salad?" Wagner withdrew his final stake from its holster and rushed at the creature, "...impaled?"

Dracula darted to the side, and in a second he was lost in the shadows. Wagner checked his strike with the wooden stake, not wanting to ruin its tip by stabbing it into the stone wall. He turned the beam of the flashlight off for a few seconds, and then on again and left it on, knowing it would burn out soon, but he needed its light. He could only just see the creature at the far end of the hall, making for the stairs to the tower. Dracula stopped and faced Wagner's light.

"Your woman will pay for your insolence!" The Count turned and fled up the stairs. Wagner could see pieces of the chute that he and Fritz had built heaped in a pile at the bottom of the steps. He wouldn't be able to use that as a quick escape if his battle with the Count went poorly. The vampire had thought of everything.

Wagner's flashlight burned out with a sharp. popping sound, and the corridor was plunged into darkness. He fumbled at this throat to pull away his neck scarf, revealing the silver cross—the last one he had. He had lost the stick he had used with his stake to make a large cross. He had no more garlic, no holy water, and the ax was gone as well. He had only one stake and the small neck cross. He gently placed the flashlight on the floor in the dark. He held the wooden stake firmly in his right hand and held his left out to feel for the wall. Once he found it, he headed to the stairwell quickly. He knew the layout of the tower well enough. He could feel his way up it in the dark with no problems. The only question would be where Dracula would be waiting for him.

Then he realized. Dracula wasn't waiting for him. He would kill Anneli, and then he would head for the top of the tower. The castle below them was on fire. Soon the blaze would consume the whole structure. But Dracula had an escape path.

He can transform into a bat, he recalled.

Dracula would simply fly away, leaving him with a dead wife and a castle burning down under him.

CHAPTER THIRTY-THREE

When Andreas Wagner rushed out of the stairwell to the top of the tower, and into the open night, he knew what he would find. The moon was up and filling the sky, seeming far closer to Earth than it could possibly be. The sky was clear and the night's fabric was punctuated with billions of brilliant stars and the hazy billow of the Milky Way.

Against the parapet wall, Dracula stood, his back to the horrendous drop down the side of the castle, and further still down the cliffside to the river far, far below in the dark. It might as well have been the drop into Hell. Anneli, her arms pinned behind her back, was held in front of him like a shield. One of his arms was across her waist, and the hand of the other was violently shoving her head to the side, exposing her pale white neck to the starshine, where it glowed like the target it was. The fiend's open jaws—his exposed fangs, clearly three times the length of the rest of his teeth—were poised to strike.

The dawn was much too far away for Wagner's taste. He stepped fully onto the roof of the castle's rear tower, with only the crenellated wall for protection from the drop on two sides to the river, and the drop to the castle roof on the others. He held the stake in his hand, but just behind his leg. He wasn't hiding it so much as hoping Dracula's attention could be placed on other things. Wagner noted that the scar from the garlic was still visible on the creature's forehead, looking angry and welting in the bright moonlight.

"How is it that you can stand the moonlight, when it is just the sun's rays reflected off the surface of the moon and back at us again?" Wagner asked, taking a step forward.

Dracula's hand moved to and tightened on Anneli's throat and Wagner stopped moving. Her eyes were telegraphing a dozen messages to him—she was sorry for getting captured, she loved him, she hated Dracula, and most importantly, she was ready for whatever he had planned.

He wished he had something planned.

He looked in her eyes and tried to project reassurance.

"I'd like to know how it is that you are not yet dead, Wagner. You are showing great resourcefulness, but it will avail you naught."

Dracula stepped from behind Anneli, still holding her by the throat, but at arm's length now, to his side. "I have the advantage, stonemason. I have your woman. You are on my land. I have all the power."

"Yes, you told me you were invincible," Wagner said. "But I think you've got that confused. I am the one who is invincible. You are the one who will die."

Wagner could see the anger rush into the Count's face, as he shoved Anneli to the side, where she fell against the parapet wall, and onto the floor. The Count brazenly stepped forward. "You have no more garlic, or I would smell it. No crosses, no weapons."

Wagner turned his body slightly, the concealed stake moving further from Dracula's view. With his free hand he reached for the small silver cross on the chain around his neck.

"I have this," he said.

Dracula hissed and swiped his hand in the air. A force like a strong wind ripped the cross and the necklace from Wagner, and it flew out over the wall to fall to the castle roof far below.

"Such a tiny thing. That hated symbol. So easy to drop. Is that all you have? That and your bravado?" Dracula swept toward him, the cape flowing out behind him in a billowing arc.

Wagner lifted the stake and made to plunge it into the Count's chest. But the fiend moved with inhuman speed, and his hand was wrapped around Wagner's wrist too soon. He twisted hard, and with titanic strength, the vampire forced him to drop the wooden stake. It rolled across the floor behind the creature.

"Invincible," the vampire scoffed. "You are nothing. You have nothing."

Dracula smashed into Wagner, forcing his back against the low parapet wall. The drop below him was to the roof of the castle, but it was still a very long way down to the moon-illuminated roofline. The Count had both of his hands wrapped around Wagner's throat. Instead of feeding on him, Wagner suspected Dracula meant to simply throttle him.

"I have two things," Wagner told him defiantly, with a croaking voice.

He brought his hands up to the front of his shirt and took hold of both sides of it, one on either side of the placket with the buttons. Grasping the fabric with the last of his strength, he tugged, ripping the fabric of the shirt asunder.

Dracula stepped back from the noise, then gasped in horror. The moonlight fell directly on Wagner's chest. The priest had spent their long hours in the room together tattooing a large cross on Wagner's chest, and the inks he used had been mixed with holy water. The moonlight made the ink gleam, and the rough, raised red bumping that had swollen around the edges of the giant tattoo looked like raw red gums around shattered teeth. The cross stretched from the top of Wagner's chest down to his navel, and the horizontal strut of the cross went just under his nipples. His chest was freshly shaved of hair, and his pale white skin served in the moonlight to emphasize the dark bluish-black of the cross pattern all the more.

Dracula cringed away, but his eyes were fixated on the cross, as if he expected it to leap off of Wagner's chest and attack him.

"I have faith," Wagner said.

Dracula's head snapped up to look at Wagner with raw hatred, as he retreated backward across the top of the tower.

Then a point on his dark suit, just over his chest pocket erupted outward, the tip of the wooden stake puncturing him from the inside. Blood gushed out of the wound and a small spatter of it landed on Wagner's bare chest. The drops that touched the holy tattoo hissed and sizzled until they were burned away. Anneli stepped from behind Dracula where she had shoved the stake through the creature's back and into its heart, forcing the wood far enough that it came out through his chest, the creature's own backward momentum assisting her thrust. Dracula looked down at the fatal wound, his eyes round and filled with surprise.

"And I have love," Wagner said softly.

Anneli crossed to him and helped him up with her small, outstretched hand, gently pulling him closer to her. They both stood and watched the life leave Dracula's face, as his body drooped and fell over onto the stone floor of the tower's rooftop. When his back hit the stones, the impact drove the stake all the way into the beast's back, and the shaft came through his chest in another gush of thick, dark blood.

EPILOGUE

The priest stood over the grave he had dug and then filled. It was not marked with a stone, for fear that there might one day be someone that would attempt to bring the undone vampire back to the world. Instead, the grave was situated at the foot of a massive ash tree. The Dutch-born priest thought the tree fitting. He would love to return to Holland, now that he was certain the Count was finished once and for all, but instead he planned to come back to this lone tree in the field for the rest of his life to ensure the creature did not again rise.

The battle must have been quite something, to hear Wagner tell it, and the priest was shocked to learn that the small, petite wife had been the one to administer the final blow. He was well pleased to discover that his ingenious tattoo had saved Wagner's life. The cross would be with the man for the rest of his days, so the priest was glad it had been useful. Wagner planned to extricate the dead Count's gold and then fill the lower levels of the castle with quick-drying concrete. The fire had destroyed much of the upper reaches of the building, but still the structure stood. Wagner would make it as inhospitable as he could before he and his wife departed the area, to return to Germany.

Good, the old man thought. *Good. We need no more nonsense from the undead.*

The grave was only a few days old, and the priest came to its side every day to ensure it remained unmolested. Already he was noticing the leaves on the tree were shriveling and dropping to the ground. Turning black like the grass around the grave. As if the Earth herself were revolting against the vampire's placement in the soil.

The priest had poured a flask of holy water on the grave each day, and he would do so again today. He had spoken the words over the soil, and planted garlic bulbs around it. He had chosen a lonely hill far from normal foot traffic, and picked the ash as a landmark so he could find his way back to it. But hopefully no one else would ever locate the unobtrusive grave.

"Well," the priest spoke aloud, in his characteristic clipped German accent. Although Dutch, he had learned to speak at the hands of a German nanny, and the dialect had stuck with him throughout his life. "We have had some times together, have we not, Count Dracula? But your days are at an end. I promised I would end you, but age and injury prevented me from doing so myself. I thought you were gone for good, but then that unsuspecting young man arrived, with his charming wife. They were looking only for a new start in life, but instead they found nothing but horror and death, because of you."

The priest paused to spit on the grave.

"You have been like a plague on the people of this land, and I swore, that as sure as my name is Abraham Van Helsing, you would one day be done. That day is today, sir."

The priest upended his flask of holy water, and poured the liquid in a steady stream onto the fresh soil of the grave. It sank into the thirsty soil immediately, leaving the surface as dry as it had appeared before.

He turned to leave and something rushed at him with darkness and screeching. He was knocked onto his back across the grave. Again a darkness blotted out the sun, as something swept at his face. He tried to hit at the thing, but it was persistent. He could feel small teeth and claws drawing blood at his neck. Then he felt his eyes being plucked out, and he began to scream.

The bat feasted on the priest's face and throat for long minutes. When it sated its gut, it flapped upward and away to the branches of the tree. Its clawed feet scrambled for a branch high in the tree's boughs, then it swung upside down and wrapped its two-foot wings around its body like a warming cloak. It shrieked once, loudly, and the forty or so other large bats hanging in the tree chittered and squeaked back at it.

As it hung, a steady drip of blood drops fell from its maw, and down to the head of the grave. The old man lay across the raw dirt of the grave, and as his body twitched and spasmed, his neck's blood ran from his ravaged Adam's apple to his shoulder and down into the ground.

The hungry earth ate the blood, and sucked it down to the waiting coffin.

ABOUT THE AUTHOR

Kane Gilmour is the bestselling co-author with thriller author Jeremy Robinson of *Ragnarok*, the fourth novel in the Jack Sigler/Chess Team series. He is also the author of *Resurrect* and *Callsign: Deep Blue*. In addition to his work in novels, Kane works with artist and creator Scott P. Vaughn on the sci-fi noir webcomic, *Warbirds of Mars*. He lives with his family in Vermont. Follow him at http://kanegilmour.com

CPSIA information can be obtained
at www.ICGtesting.com
Printed in the USA
BVOW08s1005200517
484681BV00001B/96/P